W9-CPN-934

Will She or Won't She?

"We'd better make it fast. Your answer—yes or no," Charley urged. "Will you marry me, Casey? And please don't make me ask again—it was hard enough the first time."

Casey tugged at a loose strand on the throw rug in her room. "Charley, I still don't know," she said.

"What?" he practically cried. "How can you still *not know?*"

"It's not just marrying you, which I'd be thrilled to do," Casey said. "You want me to leave school and move back to California. That's like two different decisions. And as much as I love you—"

"Are you sure?" Charley interjected.

"Charley, how many times can I tell you? I love you I love you I love you," Casey declared.

"If you really loved me, you'd say yes right away, without dragging it out," Charley finally said in a quiet voice. "If you don't want to marry me, just get up the nerve to say so. I'll be waiting to hear from you. 'Bye, Case."

NANCY DREW ON CAMPUS™

Available from ARCHWAY Paperbacks

For orders other than by individual consumers, Pocket Books grants a discount on the purchase of **10 or more** copies of single titles for special markets or premium use. For further details, please write to the Vice-President of Special Markets, Pocket Books, 1633 Broadway, New York, NY 10019-6785, 8th Floor.

For information on how individual consumers can place orders, please write to Mail Order Department, Simon & Schuster Inc., 200 Old Tappan Road, Old Tappan, NJ 07675.

Nancy Drew
on campus™ # 11

In the
Name of Love

Carolyn Keene

Eau Claire District Library

AN ARCHWAY PAPERBACK
Published by POCKET BOOKS
New York London Toronto Sydney Tokyo Singapore

108017

The sale of this book without its cover is unauthorized. If you pur-
chased this book without a cover, you should be aware that it was
reported to the publisher as "unsold and destroyed." Neither the
author nor the publisher has received payment for the sale of this
"stripped book."

This book is a work of fiction. Names, characters, places and
incidents are products of the author's imagination or are used
fictitiously. Any resemblance to actual events or locales or per-
sons, living or dead, is entirely coincidental.

AN ARCHWAY PAPERBACK *Original*

An Archway Paperback published by
POCKET BOOKS, a division of Simon & Schuster Inc.
1230 Avenue of the Americas, New York, NY 10020

Copyright © 1996 by Simon & Schuster Inc.
Produced by Mega-Books, Inc.

All rights reserved, including the right to reproduce
this book or portions thereof in any form whatsoever.
For information address Pocket Books, 1230 Avenue
of the Americas, New York, NY 10020

ISBN: 0-671-52759-2

First Archway Paperback printing July 1996

10 9 8 7 6 5 4 3 2 1

NANCY DREW, AN ARCHWAY PAPERBACK and colophon
are registered trademarks of Simon & Schuster Inc.

NANCY DREW ON CAMPUS is a trademark of
Simon & Schuster Inc.

Cover photos by Pat Hill Studio

Printed in the U.S.A.

IL 8+

In the
Name of Love

CHAPTER 1

"You're not leaving me," Jake Collins said, brushing his hand against Nancy Drew's cheek. "Are you?"

Nancy smiled, covering his strong hand with hers. "Only for a little while. I promised George we'd hang out together this morning. I've hardly seen her lately."

Nancy and Jake were sitting in a sunny spot on a grassy knoll on the Wilder University campus, sharing a late-morning breakfast of coffee and muffins.

"What about the other people you've hardly seen lately? For instance . . . *me?*" Jake asked.

Nancy kissed Jake lightly on the lips and stood up and brushed the dried leaves off her pants. "I'll call you later. Okay?"

1

"That's it?" Jake lay back on the grass and smiled up at her.

"Well, if you're going to look so pathetic . . ." Nancy knelt down and kissed Jake again. "Maybe I'll come by and visit you later. You'll be at the *Times* office, right?" She slung her backpack over her right shoulder.

Jake groaned. "Why did I ever decide to major in journalism? Nobody told me I'd have to spend every gorgeous afternoon indoors."

"Come up with a story idea that gets you outside," Nancy suggested. "You know, a major exposé of the campus quad—"

" 'Slackers at the Places They Slack'?" Jake asked, squinting up at her.

" 'And the People They Love to Slack With,' " Nancy added as the clock on the old Wilder University tower chimed ten o'clock. "Uh-oh, I'd better run. I'll call you in a couple of hours, okay?"

Jake nodded. "Say hi to George for me!"

Nancy rushed across the quad, the dry red and gold autumn leaves crackling under her feet. George Fayne was one of her best friends, and Nancy knew that George would understand why she was running late. Anyway, it wasn't as if she didn't have a reason. A very good reason: Jake.

It wasn't the first time that week that Nancy had been late for something on account of Jake. She was finding it harder and harder to tear herself away from him. When she and Jake were together, she couldn't think of anything else. Especially when he was holding her in his strong arms, looking at her with those gorgeous soft brown eyes, softly brushing her lips with a kiss.

What was the point in hurrying away from that? Nancy wondered. She'd have to be crazy.

Of course, she had just done it. But hanging out with George was just as important as spending time with Jake, Nancy told herself. George had been one of Nancy's best friends her entire life; they'd come to Wilder University from their hometown of River Heights.

The way things had been going lately, Nancy had been too busy to see much of Jake, but she was determined to find some extra hours in the day to spend with him. She didn't know where she'd find the time, but she would.

She opened the door and swept into Thayer Hall, the brisk autumn wind slamming the door closed behind her.

In Nancy's suite on the third floor, George, her curly dark hair falling around her face, was sitting in the lounge, her nose buried in a textbook.

"Hi, sorry I'm late," Nancy said with an apologetic smile as she walked into the room.

"Oh, no problem," George replied, stretching out her long legs on the couch. "But I'm glad you showed up—I was actually starting to *study*."

Nancy laughed. "No! Anything but that!" she joked, tossing her backpack on a lounge chair.

"It's horrible," George said. "But it's a must when you're in calculus. I don't know why you're late, but I'm betting from that extremely happy look on your face that it has something to do with Jake. Am I right?"

Nancy nodded.

"So things are going well between you guys?" George asked.

"Better than well," Nancy said. "In fact, things are great. How about with you and Will?"

George had been seeing Will Blackfeather, a sophomore, since her first weeks at Wilder.

"Everything's fine," George said, leaning back on the couch. "Wonderful, fantastic, stupendous . . . Am I getting too carried away?"

"No, you're not getting carried away." Nancy laughed. "Not for someone who's in love."

George grinned. "So, besides seeing Jake, what else is up with you?"

"Well, I have a ton of stuff to do, as usual. Remember how I wanted to get involved with Helping Hands?" Nancy asked. Helping Hands was a local organization that paired Wilder students as big brothers or big sisters with teenagers in single parent families.

"Of course I remember," George said. "You've been trying to get hooked up with a little sister, right?"

Nancy nodded. "I'm meeting her tomorrow for the first time! Her name's Anna Pederson. I can't wait." Growing up, Nancy had been an only child—she'd always wondered how it would feel to have a younger brother or sister. She was excited about having a chance to meet and work with Anna, who was twelve.

"Do you know anything about her?" George asked.

"Not that much," Nancy admitted, "but I'm sure we'll work it out. The only problem will be finding enough time to spend with her. I don't know why, but so far this has been the craziest week of the whole semester. On top of all my regular classwork—which is enough for a small army—Gail wants me to cover the World Arts and Crafts Show at the Student Union on Friday." Gail Gardeski was editor-in-chief of the *Wilder Times,* the college newspaper where Nancy and Jake were both reporters.

"And?" George prompted.

"And what?" Nancy asked.

"And what about Jake? Do you have any time for him?"

"What do you think?" Nancy said. "Don't

you always find time for Will?" When you're in love, there's always time. She touched her lips, remembering Jake's soft kiss. She couldn't wait for the next one.

"Bess," Casey Fontaine whispered. She grabbed the sleeve of Bess Marvin's red sweatshirt as Bess passed her in the Rockhausen Library stacks. "I've been looking all over for you."

"Oh, hi, Casey!" Bess grinned, her blue eyes flashing even in the dim fluorescent library light. "What's up?"

"Let's go over here." Casey gestured to a corner nook, where she felt they could get some privacy. What she had to tell Bess wasn't something she wanted anyone else to know. But she was dying to tell somebody—and Casey knew she could trust Bess, a fellow Kappa sorority member, with a secret. Casey lived in the same suite as Nancy Drew, one of Bess's best friends.

"So? What's so important?" Bess demanded. "You look so intense."

"Well, you're not going to believe this," Casey began.

"Wait—don't tell me. You landed a hot new role in a movie! And you're leaving Wilder!" Bess guessed.

"No," Casey said. "Nothing like that." If Bess only knew! Her news had nothing to do with her acting career. Casey had starred on a television series called *The President's Daughter* before she left Hollywood to come to Wilder.

"Casey, spit it out already!" Bess cried, her voice echoing in the cavernous stacks.

Several whispers of "Shh!" came at them from all directions.

"Whoops. Sorry," Bess whispered, curling her blond hair back behind her ear.

"Just don't shout out what I'm about to tell you. Promise?" Casey said.

Bess sighed. "Yes, now spill it."

"Charley proposed to me before he left town," Casey said slowly.

Bess clapped her hand over her mouth and stared at Casey. "Proposed? As in marriage? As in . . . walking down the aisle? You're kidding!"

"No. He wants me to marry him, drop out of Wilder, and move back to Los Angeles," Casey explained. Saying it out loud to someone else made the decision seem even more serious. Get married? Drop out of Wilder? But she'd just started—and the reason she'd come to Wilder was to experience something different from the L.A. scene.

She loved Charley with all her heart. She'd met him when they were costars in *The President's Daughter,* and they'd been dating exclusively since then. She didn't want to see anyone else, and she knew she was devoted to Charley.

But she was also devoted to pursuing her education, especially in a place like Wilder, where she could just be herself and not worry about tabloid photographers snapping her picture everywhere she went.

"So . . . what did you say?" Bess asked.

"I said I'd have to think about it." Casey shrugged her shoulders. "What else could I say? I was totally surprised."

"I see what you mean," Bess said. "But what have you decided *since* then?"

Casey threw up her hands. "That's just it! I can't decide. It's such a major life change, and I feel like I have so much going on, I don't even have time to really think it through."

"Don't you want to marry Charley? You guys really love each other, right?" Bess asked.

"Yes. We do," Casey said. "And in a way, that's what makes it so hard. Because this decision could either bring us closer together or . . . I don't know."

"Well, it's not an ultimatum," Bess said. "Charley's still going to love you, no matter what you decide."

"I guess so," Casey mused. She thought of Charley, picturing how earnest he'd looked when he'd asked her to marry him and how sad she'd felt when they had to say goodbye.

She definitely wanted to marry him someday, but now? She just wasn't sure.

"Hey, have you talked to Bess today?" Nancy asked. She and George had been talking in the lounge for about half an hour.

"I think I talked to her, but I'm not sure," George said. "I called her room, and this person who sounds like Bess answered. But then she said she was going to the *library.*"

"Hmm." Nancy drummed her fingers against the arm of the couch. "Doesn't sound like Bess to me." Then she and George started laughing. Studying was always the last thing on Bess's mind.

The door to the suite opened, and Dawn Steiger walked down the hall toward them, followed by Bill Graham. Both Dawn and Bill were resident advisers in Thayer.

"What's up, guys?" Nancy asked.

George pointed to the stack of neon green posters Bill was carrying. "Ooh. Don't tell me—Thayer's putting on a major party this weekend!"

"Not exactly," Dawn said. Her long blond hair was pulled back into a ponytail, and she was wearing jeans and a maroon Wilder sweatshirt.

Bill held up one of the posters for George and Nancy to look at. The Buddy System Works—Use It! the posters proclaimed in

large black letters. Increase Campus Safety—
Don't Walk Alone At Night.

"Oh, is this a campaign across campus?"
Nancy asked. "One of those public service
things you guys promote?"

"It's a campaign, but it's not something we
planned," Dawn said, sitting on the arm of the
couch. She rested the stapler on her knee. "It's
kind of last minute. After the fact."

"What do you mean?" George asked.
"There's a reason you're doing this today?"

Bill let out a loud sigh. "Unfortunately. We
got some really bad news this morning."

"What happened?" George asked. "Was
somebody hurt?"

Dawn nodded. "There was an attack outside
Thayer. It was Reva."

"Reva *Ross?*" George leaned forward on
the couch, incredulous. Reva was one of the
women in Nancy's suite. George didn't know
her well, but Nancy had spent a lot of time
with her.

"Is she okay?" Nancy asked.

"Fortunately, yes," Bill told her. "She was
mugged, but the guy didn't hurt her. I mean,
he might have bruised her a little, but nothing
serious. She's fine."

"Wow." George couldn't believe it. "That's
terrible."

"You're not kidding," Nancy agreed. "I

can't believe it happened to someone from our suite."

"Yeah, neither can I," Dawn said. "I thought Wilder was a pretty safe place. Anyway, we're putting up posters all over the dorm to let everyone know they should be careful."

"So . . . where's Reva now?" Nancy asked tentatively, pulling her boxy cardigan sweater tighter around her.

"She went to stay with Andy last night," Dawn said.

Andy Rodriguez and Reva had been dating for a while now. George knew Andy well because he was Will's roommate. Funny, she thought. Will hadn't mentioned anything about Reva when she'd spoken to him that morning. He must not know yet; or maybe Reva didn't want other people to know. "Has Reva reported this to the police or anything?" George asked.

"Last night after they checked her out at the hospital," Bill said. "The police interviewed her, I guess, and she told them what she knew about it. Which wasn't much, because it all happened really fast."

"Whew. Mugged," Nancy said. "It must have been awful."

"Yeah. She was pretty shaken up. Andy picked her up at the station after the police took her statement," Dawn explained.

George shook her head. "I still can't believe it. Why did this have to happen to Reva?"

"More like, why does this have to happen to *anyone*," Dawn added. "If you're not safe at Wilder, where *are* you safe?"

George shrugged. "I don't know. But I think I'll go over to Will and Andy's to see how she's doing. Want to come along?" she asked Nancy.

"I really want to see Reva but I should go over to the *Times* office. Jake's there, and I want to see if they're handling the story," Nancy said. "That is, if they even know about it yet. I'll ask Gail to put something in about everyone taking extra safety precautions."

George nodded. "Good idea."

"Yeah. If they could put something in the paper, that'd be great. I mean, the more we can get the word out, the better," Dawn agreed.

"In the meantime, we've got posters to put up all over the dorm," Bill said, adjusting the stack in his arms.

"Then we'll see you later," George said. Bill and Dawn took off, and she turned to Nancy. "Poor Reva."

"Poor Reva is right!" Nancy looked concerned. "I can't believe she was attacked. Thank goodness it was only a mugging. What if—"

"Don't even think it," George said. But she was already thinking it. Getting mugged was bad enough, but what if something even worse had happened to Reva?

12

CHAPTER 2

Reva turned over on the bed, her arms wrapped tightly around a pillow. Andy's apartment was so peaceful, with the late morning light streaming in through the window. He was making coffee, and the smell drifted from the kitchen into his bedroom, making Reva feel that she was back at home. She felt that she was being taken care of.

Still, as hard as she tried, she couldn't forget the terror of being pushed up against the wall and having her wallet yanked from her backpack and her gold bracelet snapped off her wrist as if it were nothing more than kite string. She hadn't even seen the guy, and it had lasted only half a minute, but that half minute was long enough to turn everything upside down in her life. She'd always felt com-

13

Eau Claire District Library

fortable going places by herself; now the thought of leaving Andy's apartment for her morning classes made her shake. She was turning into a wimp.

"Hey. You okay?" Andy walked into the room, carrying two mugs of coffee. He set one mug down on the small bedside table and handed the other to Reva.

"Thanks." Reva sat up and smiled slightly, holding the steaming mug. She sipped a little of the coffee, then put the mug down on the floor.

"Well? How are you feeling?" Andy asked, reaching out to touch Reva's long black hair.

Reva shrugged, putting her hand on top of Andy's. She couldn't lie to Andy. "Not great. Thanks for letting me stay with you last night, though. It helped." Andy had picked her up at the police station and driven her back to his apartment. Then, all night, he'd just held her while she lay on top of his bed.

"I'm just glad I was here when you called," Andy said. He sipped his coffee. "If only I'd been there when—"

Reva put her finger on Andy's lips. "Don't say it. Don't feel guilty about it, okay?"

"Still, if I'd been there, I could have flattened that guy. I could have—ooh." Andy shuddered. "What a jerk! Why attack you—for some spare change and a bracelet that means nothing to him?"

"I couldn't care less about my wallet," Reva said. "I mean, it's not like I had any credit cards or anything. Just a couple of bills. But the bracelet . . ." She looked at Andy sadly. "That really meant a lot to me." Andy had given her the gold bracelet with a heart-shaped charm engraved with a tiny *R*. She loved the bracelet, and wearing it reminded her of how much she loved Andy. Now Andy's gift belonged to some creep—if he hadn't already pawned it.

"Me, too. But don't worry, I'll get you another one. Just not right away," Andy said, looking worried.

Reva didn't want Andy to rush out and buy her another bracelet. She knew he couldn't afford the first one. But she didn't want to say anything that might make him feel worse than he already did about her attack.

Anyway, she couldn't hole up in Andy's apartment all day. Besides, going to classes would help to take her mind off the attack.

Reva looked over at Andy. Sure, it sounded like a good plan, but Reva didn't want to leave Andy's side. "Would you mind walking over to Thayer with me?" she asked. "I need to change my clothes and pick up some books."

"Sure," Andy said, nodding. He set his coffee mug down. "Whatever you want—I'm there for you. But first"—he scooted over on the bed and wrapped his arms around Reva's waist—"promise me you'll let me walk you everywhere from now on."

Reva felt the tension in her body dissipate as Andy squeezed her tighter. She leaned closer to him, putting her arms around his strong shoulders. "You can't be with me all the time."

"I can't?" Andy ran his fingers down the back of her neck. "Who says I can't?" He kissed her lightly on the neck.

"Well—maybe we can work *something* out," Reva said as Andy held her close.

Jake stared at the blank computer screen in front of him, his black cowboy boots propped on either side of it. He was writing an article, but so far had only three words. The title: "Tuition Will Rise." With a topic that depressing, no wonder he was having trouble writing.

He heard the office door close, and a few seconds later, Nancy was standing in front of his desk.

"Missed me more than you thought, didn't you?" He grinned at her.

"Yes," she said. "But that's not why I'm here."

Jake stopped smiling. The look on Nancy's face was so serious. "What's up?" he asked.

"You didn't hear?" she answered.

"Hear what?" Jake put his hand on Nancy's arm. "What's wrong?"

Nancy came around to the side of his desk. "Somebody mugged Reva last night. The guy made off with her wallet, some jewelry . . ."

"You're kidding." Jake exhaled. "Here on campus?"

Nancy nodded. "Right outside our *dorm.*"

Jake shook his head in disbelief and anger. Where was campus security last night? he thought. "What time did it happen?" he asked Nancy.

"I don't know exactly. Late, I guess," Nancy said. "I haven't talked to her yet—she's at Andy's. But I want to see her and find out more, and maybe we can get some information from the police. I think we should tell Gail and get an article in the paper about it."

"Good idea. We can warn everyone to watch out." Jake tapped his pencil against his keyboard. "In fact, on top of the article, maybe we can print a list of tips on how to stay safe on campus."

"That's exactly why I came over here," Nancy said. "That and wanting to see you. Hearing about Reva, I suddenly had to be near you. You know what I mean?"

Jake nodded. "Of course. That's what I'm here for." He stood up and pulled her close.

"I thought you were here to write your articles," Nancy said, a sly smile turning up the corners of her mouth as she looked at him.

"Isn't that what you told me, oh, about an hour ago?"

"Well, can I help it if you're distracting me? Keeping me from my work? Oh—speaking of which . . ." He released her and rustled through the stack of papers scattered on his desk.

"Organized as usual?" Nancy teased him.

"Hey, when you have a system that works, you don't mess with it," Jake replied. "Everything I need is in this pile. Somewhere."

"Uh-huh." Nancy smiled. "I'll believe it when I see it."

"Aha!" he cried. "Here it is. See, I told you." He fished a few pamphlets out of the middle of the pile. "Remember the Citizens for White Purity organization I wrote an editorial on?"

Nancy nodded. "Sure, that creepy group that's started up on campus the last few weeks."

"Well, I've been checking into the organization some more because I want to do a more in-depth article on them," Jake said. "I picked up some of their pamphlets on campus." He held one out to Nancy.

She stared at the cover. " 'White Is Right, White Is Might'?" she read out loud, making a face.

"It gets worse," Jake warned her. He still couldn't get over the negative, inflammatory language in the group's pamphlets. The Citizens for White Purity organization believed in the complete separation of racial and religious groups and in keeping the white race "pure."

"This stuff's disgusting!" Nancy said as she read the pamphlet.

Jake nodded. "Yeah. I especially like the part where they encourage people to *act* on their beliefs."

Nancy put the pamphlet back on his desk. "I'd always heard about groups like this, but I guess I thought they were far from anyplace I was. How big a group is it?"

"Bigger than I thought," Jake told her.

"Really?" A wrinkle of concern creased Nancy's forehead.

"Listen to this." Jake picked up the pad of paper on his desk and reviewed his notes. "Just in the last few months there was a synagogue in the next town that was defaced, some hate messages sprayed on a professor's house, and a couple of people in the Asian-American student organization were harassed by skinheads."

"That's a lot to have happened," Nancy commented pensively.

"No kidding. This group has been on campus using these pamphlets to recruit people to join them. I also found out that the leader of CWP is a guy named Wayne French," Jake explained.

Nancy stared at the pamphlets, then up at Jake. "Wait a second. Citizens for White Purity. You know, Reva's African American. You don't think they could have been involved in the attack on her last night? You said they're urging people to take action."

"True, they are," Jake said. "But you said she was mugged, right? And someone did take her wallet."

"And her gold bracelet," Nancy said.

"If this group was involved, they'd be more likely to try to scare her or leave a message or something," Jake reasoned. "Stealing doesn't seem to be their style."

"Maybe not," Nancy said with a sigh.

"I think that the attack on Reva was an isolated incident," Jake said. "Somebody needed money and saw her as an opportunity. As much as we don't want to think about it, muggings do happen every day."

"I know, but at Wilder? I thought it was so safe here," Nancy said.

"It ought to be," Jake said. "You know, for this follow-up article on the CWP, I was planning to find Wayne French and talk to him."

"Good idea," Nancy said. "You know, I'd like to talk to him myself. Just to see what makes someone like that—"

"The way he is. I know." Jake nodded. "I'm going to write a complete exposé on their lousy little hate group. I want to make sure everyone knows exactly what their message is and what they're capable of."

"Well, be careful," Nancy warned.

"You, too," Jake said. "I don't want what happened to Reva to happen to you. Or to anyone else, for that matter. In fact, maybe I shouldn't let you out of my sight."

"Oh, really? And how are you going to do that?" Nancy asked.

Jake pulled Nancy onto his lap and held her tight, his arms wrapped around her waist. "Well, we could start with lunch . . ."

"I thought you had to finish your article," Nancy said. "Actually, first we should write the article about Reva's attack. Then we can go to lunch."

"Sure. We'll get that article done eventually," Jake said. "But right now this seems like a lot more fun."

"My very own private security guard," Nancy murmured as Jake kissed her neck. "Hmm . . . I could get used to this."

"It's impossible!" Bess Marvin cried, tossing a worn T-shirt across her room toward the closet. She bit her lip and turned to her roommate, Leslie King, who was sitting at her desk. "Sorry. I know you're trying to study."

Leslie turned around. "It's okay. Getting our room clean is just as important."

Bess smiled. In the past she would have

cringed at a remark like that from Leslie. She and Leslie had spent the first several weeks of living together disagreeing about everything. But lately, since Leslie had decided to ease up on pressuring herself to study all the time, she and Bess had worked out a much better living situation. They weren't best friends yet, but they weren't enemies, either.

"I don't know how it gets like this so fast!" Bess complained, opening her arms wide to indicate the mess. "It's like some kind of weird clean-space-eating bacteria."

"I'll say." Leslie surveyed the room with a serious look, then laughed. "Come on—we can do it together." She stood up and walked over to the CD player on Bess's dresser. "Maybe some music will help motivate us."

Bess almost fell over. Leslie offering to help? And putting on loud dance music? "You're feeling okay, aren't you?" she asked. Other than being a hundred percent out of character, that is, she added to herself.

"I feel great." Leslie grabbed a pile of clothes off the floor. "Laundry?"

"Laundry," Bess agreed with a puzzled expression on her face as she watched Leslie fling clothes across the room. Leslie King was actually helping Bess clean *her* side of the room? Since when? "Leslie, are you sure you're not overdoing your therapy sessions?" she asked.

Leslie laughed. "If you keep making fun of me, I'll stop."

Bess grinned at her. "I think you're making remarkable progress. Now, the dry cleaning goes here, and the sweaters—"

The ringing of the telephone interrupted Bess. Leslie grabbed the phone off her bed before it could ring twice. "Hello? Oh, hi." Leslie's face turned pink.

Who could that be? Bess wondered as Leslie let out a light giggle. Leslie wasn't acting like herself at all.

"Eight o'clock Saturday sounds good," Leslie said. "Okay. See you then, Nathan." She hung up the telephone receiver with a sigh.

"What's going on?" Bess asked.

"Oh, not much." Leslie shrugged as she wound a strand of her long brown hair around her finger. "Actually, it's just this date that I have."

"Leslie, I've never seen you actually *blush* before. Nathan must be important," Bess said.

"Okay, so I'm hopelessly obvious." Leslie sank onto her bed. "And totally unprepared."

"What's to prepare?" Bess shrugged. "You pick out an outfit, he picks you up, *voilà*. The date."

"I haven't been on a date in so long, not since high school," Leslie admitted. "It's so embarrassing."

"Don't be embarrassed," Bess said. "So you

23

haven't been on a date since you got to Wilder—so what?"

"Well, even the dates I did have in high school weren't exactly romantic. They were more like study dates."

"Oh. I see." Bess tossed a few scraps of paper into the wastebasket. "Well then, I'll just have to help you get ready, won't I?"

"Would you?" Leslie asked eagerly.

"Sure. Of course, in terms of helping you, there *is* a fee."

Leslie gave her a skeptical look. "Fee?"

"Oh, don't worry. My advice comes cheap," Bess replied. "All you have to do is—help me finish cleaning my side of the room!"

Reva stuffed her notebook back into her black canvas knapsack and started to walk out of the lecture hall. Listening to the lecture in her African American literature class for the past hour had been very relaxing—almost enough to take her mind off the night before.

Reva had just taken a step out into the hall when somebody grabbed hold of her arm.

She jumped back, throwing the hand off and holding her knapsack out in front of her as a shield. Her heart was beating double time.

"Reva! Relax, it's only me," a deep voice said.

Reva looked up. When she saw who was standing in front of her, she felt like collapsing with relief. It was Darrell Jones, a computer technician on campus. Reva had met him a few weeks earlier when he came to fix her computer. He was tall and very good-looking, with rich brown skin and eyes and short black hair.

"Hey, Darrell," she said. "Sorry—I guess I'm a little on edge today. Too much coffee or something." She laughed nervously. If only she *was* suffering from caffeine overload, she'd be happy.

"You don't have to pretend with me," Darrell said, giving her a sympathetic look. "I heard what happened to you last night. That's why I'm here. Actually—I wanted to make sure you were okay, see if I could do anything to help."

"But how—how did you know?" Reva asked. So far, she thought only the women in her suite knew, besides Andy and Will.

Darrell shrugged a little sheepishly. "I went to see you this morning, and Eileen told me about it and which class I could find you in. I hope I haven't invaded your space or anything."

"No, it's okay." But Reva felt embarrassed. Darrell had asked her out a few times after he'd fixed her computer, but she hadn't been interested because she was seeing Andy. Darrell had finally met Andy recently at the Black & White Nights, and since then he'd accepted the fact that Reva and Andy were serious about each other.

"So how are you? Did he hurt you?" Darrell asked in a soft voice.

Reva shook her head. "Not really."

"Good. I'm glad." Darrell smiled faintly. "I know it must be really awful to go through something like that, though. So on the way over, I picked this up for you." He reached into his denim jacket pocket and pulled out a small wrapped box.

"Darrell, you didn't need to do this," Reva said, genuinely surprised. She wondered if maybe Darrell didn't understand about her wanting to be friends only.

He placed the box in her hand. "It's nothing, really. Just something to make you feel better. You don't even have to open it now."

"Well . . ."

"Look, can I give you a ride somewhere?" Darrell asked. "Your next class? Back to Thayer?"

Reva didn't want to encourage him by accepting a ride, but she couldn't wait to get back to the quiet safety of her own room and hang out with Eileen. She hadn't even realized how tense she was about walking around campus. "Okay. Thanks."

"Great! Let's go." Darrell walked to the door and held it open for Reva.

I wonder what the gift is, Reva thought, turning the box over in her hand.

CHAPTER 3

"But, Dad—this weekend is so sudden!" Stephanie Keats cried. "You and Kiki can't come to visit me on such short notice. It's not fair. I'm already busy this weekend. I've got practically a dozen plans, not to mention *dates*."

Casey sighed and rolled onto her side. She was trying to study, but with Stephanie talking on the phone in their room for the past half hour, it was getting harder and harder to concentrate.

Not that Casey could ask Stephanie to continue her conversation later, when Casey wasn't studying. Stephanie was accustomed to having everything exactly her way.

"Daddy, that's impossible," Stephanie said. "You want me to go camping in Montana instead of lying on the beach in the Bahamas over the holidays?"

"Casey! Telephone!" Eileen O'Connor called, knocking lightly on Casey's open door. Eileen, Reva's roommate, was also a member of the Kappas.

"Thanks." Casey dropped her textbook on the floor and stood up, stretching her arms above her head.

"It's Charley," Eileen said as Casey walked out into the lounge. "He says he tried to get through to you on your line for an hour or more."

Casey smiled. "No, really?" Eileen laughed as Casey picked up the phone receiver off the couch. "Hi—sorry. Stephanie's been totally monopolizing the phone all morning."

"She can be so annoying that way," Charley said. "Have you ever thought about getting call waiting?"

Casey laughed. "No, but I might. Anyway, what's up? How are you?" She smiled at Eileen, who was sitting in a chair on the other side of the lounge, casually reading. Couldn't Eileen take the hint and give her a little privacy?

"Well, I'm great," Charley replied. "Except that I feel like I'm sitting on pins and needles ever since I left. Have you thought any more about what I asked you?"

"Of course I have," Casey said. "I mean, I

haven't been able to think about anything else, which is really bad, considering I have a test on Friday." She glanced up at Ginny Yuen, who had walked into the suite, and waved.

Ginny waved back. "Hi, Casey!" she whispered before going into the room she shared with Liz Bader.

"So? What did you decide? You're killing me here, Case."

Casey twirled the phone cord around her ring finger. She'd been thinking about Charley's proposal constantly, but it wasn't helping her come up with an answer.

"Charley, you know how much I love you," she began in a whisper. She really didn't want Eileen to hear about all this until she was sure what she wanted.

"Uh-oh. This doesn't sound good," Charley complained. "This sounds like you're about to dump me."

"No—I don't mean it like that! As if I would ever break up with you!" Casey quickly added in a soft voice. "It's just that ... getting married is such a huge step. And I don't know if I want to move back to L.A."

"Why not?" Charley asked.

"Because the whole reason I left was to go to Wilder and—"

"So, you can transfer to a school here," Charley said. "It's easy—people do it all the time."

29

"True," Casey said. "But I *like* it here."

Eileen shifted in her chair, knocking a pen to the floor. "Sorry!" she whispered.

Casey forced herself to concentrate on Charley. "You know that once I'm in L.A., it'll be harder to resist acting offers. And I'm definitely sure I don't want to go back into that just yet," she whispered.

"I know," Charley said, sounding defensive. "I mean, we've talked about all that."

Casey could tell from the tone in Charley's voice that he was getting irritated with her. He wanted an answer, and she didn't have an answer—yet. What was worse, she didn't feel comfortable discussing something so private in the middle of the lounge, with Eileen sitting there and everyone else walking in and out. "Charley, this is really hard to talk about on the telephone. I'm in the lounge and—"

"You just don't want to talk about it," Charley said. "Period."

"No, I do—" Casey began to protest.

"No, you don't," Charley replied curtly. "Listen, you know where I stand. I'm waiting to hear how you feel about it. So when you're actually ready to give me an answer, call me." He hung up the phone.

The dial tone buzzed in Casey's ear as she glanced nervously at Eileen.

"How's Charley?" Eileen asked.

"Charley's . . . great." Casey dropped the receiver back into its cradle. She wasn't sure what had just happened between them, but she was pretty sure it wasn't good.

Didn't Charley know that she couldn't make a serious decision like that overnight?

"Reva!" Nancy called across the parking lot outside Thayer. Nancy had been on her way back to the suite when she spotted Reva getting out of a blue car.

"Hi, Nancy!" Reva said.

"How are you?" Nancy asked. She glanced at Reva's friend, a tall guy whom Nancy didn't recognize.

"Fine. A little nervous, maybe," Reva said, shifting her nylon knapsack to her other shoulder. "Have you met Darrell?"

"No." Nancy shook her head, then held out her hand. "Hi. I'm Nancy Drew."

"Darrell Jones. It's nice to meet you," he said, shaking her hand with a firm grip.

"Darrell gave me a ride back from lit class," Reva said. "He's a technician for Campus Computers. He rescued me once from the brink of disaster when my hard disk crashed," Reva explained.

"Something I'm hoping I never have to face," Nancy said. "Well, it's great to meet you, Darrell. I'll definitely call you in case there's an emergency with my computer."

"I hope you never have to," Darrell said.

"Then again, if computers didn't malfunction, I'd be out of a job, so . . ." He shrugged. "Whatever goes wrong, let's hope it's nothing serious." He grinned at Nancy.

"Agreed," she said with a laugh.

"Well, I should probably get going, Reva," Darrell said, opening the car door.

"Thanks for the ride," Reva said. "Really—that was great."

"No problem. Anytime, okay?" Darrell slid into the driver's seat and closed the door. When he did, several flecks of rust and paint fluttered to the ground. Darrell shook his head. "This thing's falling apart right before my eyes. I got into an accident, and I've been trying to fix the dents in the back by myself."

Nancy looked around at the back of the small blue car. "What happened?"

"It's too stupid to even talk about," Darrell said, shaking his head, "but all my fault, unfortunately, so my insurance company won't pay for anything."

Reva pointed to the backseat, which was piled with several cans of touch-up spray paint, rolls of duct tape, and various wrenches and other tools. "Are you going to repaint it or something?"

"If I can get the dents and scrapes hammered out, then sure I'll repaint it," Darrell joked. "But I don't think I'll live that long!"

Nancy laughed. "I have three words for you, Darrell."

"Give up now?" Darrell joked.

Reva grinned. "Good idea!"

Nancy smiled at her. It was nice to know that Reva felt relaxed enough to have a little fun, even after what had happened. "Actually, I was thinking more along the lines of—auto body shop. There are people who do this for a living, you know."

"I know," Darrell said. "But I can't really afford it. Unless someone I just met who has a computer suddenly started having major trouble with say . . . everything? And they needed hours and hours of technical support?"

"Forget about it. You're not even *touching* my keyboard!" Nancy grabbed Reva's arm, and they ran off toward Thayer, laughing.

It was Wednesday evening, and George and Will were standing in front of her dorm, Jamison Hall. She released Will's hand and turned to go inside. "I guess this is goodbye. For the next twelve hours, anyway."

She looked up into Will's face, at his bold cheekbones and dark brown eyes. As many times as she looked at Will, she still couldn't believe he was her boyfriend and that he loved her and she loved him. It had all happened so fast that sometimes she felt as if she was still catching her breath.

"Do we have to?" Will took George's hand in his again.

"Yes," George said with a laugh. "Or else we're going to become permanently attached at the hip."

Will wrapped his arms around George's waist and pulled her closer. "And that would be . . . a bad thing?" He traced her chin with his finger, then kissed her on the lips.

"I'm trying to remember," George said. "I think it's supposed to be a bad idea, but I don't know why." She brushed Will's cheek with a soft kiss.

"You know . . . I hate to say this, because I know you're perfectly capable of taking care of yourself," Will said, staring intently at her. "But after what happened to Reva last night, I feel really worried about leaving you all alone."

"I'm not all alone," George pointed out. "There's my roommate, Pam, not to mention a hundred other girls in my dorm."

"I know that, logically," Will admitted, "but I just hate the thought of you walking across campus by yourself or going out jogging."

"I don't run at night, you know that," George said. "And I plan to be extra careful when I do run during the day."

Will sighed. "I'd still feel better if you stayed with me for a few days."

"Will, I'd love to do that—I really would"—

George kissed him gently on the cheek—"but I can't. Stop worrying!" George said, her hand on his arm. "I can take care of myself."

"All right," Will said reluctantly. "But can I at least walk you upstairs? Maybe we could spend a little more time together tonight—"

"You know how much I'd love to spend all night with you," George said, smiling at Will. "But I have over fifty pages to read for my western civ class, not to mention studying for calculus. And if you're around, I know I won't get anything done."

"Me? Interfere?" Will acted offended. "Never."

"Sure, unless you wanted to, say, *kiss* me or something." George raised her eyebrows.

"All you have to do is ask." Will hugged her close and their lips met in a long, passionate kiss.

"Good night," George said, taking a few steps toward the door.

Will shook his head. "You're heartless. You know that, don't you?"

"I'll see you tomorrow, first thing," George promised. " 'Bye!" She opened the dorm door and slipped inside. Didn't Will know it was as hard for her to leave him after a kiss like that as it was for him to leave her? She'd stay with him all night, if she could.

But she couldn't think of one professor who'd accept "hopelessly in love" as an excuse for a late paper. Sometimes classes really got in the way of college, George thought, smiling to herself as she took the stairs to her room two at a time.

"So, are you doing as well as you seem to be?" Nancy asked Reva. They were sitting in their lounge, sharing a bowl of microwave popcorn with Casey. "Because considering it only happened about twenty-four hours ago, I think you're doing fantastically well."

Reva shrugged. "I don't know *how* I feel. Sort of relaxed, actually. I mean, I don't feel like taking a walk by myself or anything! But I'm not really nervous."

"Good," Casey said. "You shouldn't be. I mean, we should all look out, of course. But it really sounds to me like the guy from last night just wanted some cash. He got your wallet—end of story."

"He also got the gold bracelet Andy gave me," Reva said with a dejected sigh. "That's what really upset me." Reva was glad she had friends like Nancy and Casey to talk things through. She grabbed a handful of popcorn and tossed a kernel into her mouth.

"I wonder why you had to have such rotten luck," Nancy mused. "You know, why this guy picked on you."

"It was dark, and I was alone." Reva

shrugged. "Classic situation we're always told to avoid."

"Right," Nancy said. "It's in all those pamphlets they gave us when we got here. But you never think it'll actually happen, and definitely not to you."

"You know, it's so ridiculous. We shouldn't have to think about whether we go out alone or where or what time," Casey declared fiercely. "This is a small town, not some major city like New York—"

"Or Los Angeles. At least we don't have earthquakes," Nancy said, shrugging.

Reva laughed. She finally felt comfortable enough to slip out of her jacket, which she'd been wearing almost as a security blanket ever since class. As she took it off, the box Darrell had given her dropped out of the pocket. "Oh, I almost forgot. Darrell gave me this to cheer me up," she told Nancy with a smile.

"He was nice," Nancy said. "And pretty funny, too."

"Yeah, I like him," Reva said. She opened the small box and peered inside. "What?" she mumbled, picking up a tiny gold bracelet almost exactly like the one that had been stolen the night before, except that it didn't have a tiny heart charm.

"You know," Nancy said, staring at the bracelet. "That kind of looks like the one that was taken from you."

Reva nodded. "Yes, isn't that weird? I guess Darrell noticed my bracelet before. He came by the dorm this morning to see me, and Eileen told him what happened. She must have mentioned my bracelet getting taken."

"But your bracelet was a special gift from Andy, right?" Casey said.

Reva nodded.

"I think it's a little much for a guy who's supposed to be a friend to give you something that nice," Casey said. "Isn't a gold bracelet kind of an extravagant gift from someone who's only trying to cheer you up?"

"I guess he just wanted to replace the one that was stolen," Reva replied. "Maybe he didn't stop to think about how appropriate it was."

"Sounds like he wants to be more than a friend," Casey said.

Reva nodded. "We've talked about that, and I thought he understood where I was coming from. Maybe he hasn't really accepted it, though."

Nancy handed Reva the bracelet. "He was probably just trying to be supportive and didn't realize that this was going overboard. I don't think he meant to cause a problem."

"Oh, no," Reva said. "I'm sure he didn't."

"Must be rough having two gorgeous guys giving you jewelry," Nancy teased her.

Reva shook her head. "Ha-ha. Very funny."

She opened the cardboard box and laid the bracelet back on the white cotton layer. "I'll have to give this back to him. If I accept it, he might think I'm interested in him, which I'm not. I'm only interested in Andy."

"Speaking of Andy—I haven't seen him around lately," Casey said. "How's he doing?"

"Great," Reva said. "You guys wouldn't believe how sweet and supportive he was last night."

"Of course we would," Nancy said, smiling. "Andy's a great guy."

"Yes, he is," Reva said, thinking of how warm and protected she'd felt in Andy's arms that morning, before she had to leave his apartment. She wouldn't do anything to jeopardize their relationship.

The first chance she got, she would give the bracelet back to Darrell. Maybe I can track him down through Campus Computers, she thought. In the meantime, she was going to carry the bracelet around with her, in case she ran into him. She didn't want his gift to cause problems for anybody—but especially not for her and Andy.

CHAPTER 4

Thursday morning George sleepily pulled her sweatshirt over her head, then sat down on her roommate's bed. "Come on, Pam. Time for our morning run." George started tying her sneakers.

Pam groaned.

"Spoken like a true champion," George said, pinching Pam's foot.

"Hey. No fair," Pam grumbled, her head buried underneath the covers.

"Come on," George urged. "Lazy bones, up and at 'em."

Pam's face emerged from beneath her comforter. "Sorry, George. I'm exhausted. Jamal and I were out so late last night—"

"I know, I didn't even hear you come in," George said. "What were you doing? Or shouldn't I ask?" She wiggled her eyebrows at Pam.

"Oh, my gosh. I didn't tell you what happened on Tuesday." Pam sat up in bed, propping her back against a pillow.

"No. I've barely seen you all week, remember?" George reminded her.

"Right. Well, I've been at Jamal's place because I was so freaked out about what happened." Pam stretched. "Jamal and I were at the Underground, okay? And we're just sitting there, having a good time, keeping totally to ourselves. Then we get up to leave, and this *jerk* starts yelling things at us about how we don't belong there because we're black, and—"

"You're kidding! That's horrible," George said, staring at Pam with concern.

"Tell me about it." Pam nodded. "So then Jamal decides he's not going to ignore them and walk away, like I would have. And he practically gets into a fistfight with the ringleader, a huge skinhead with steel-toed boots. I pulled him away."

George shook her head. "How can this stuff happen at the Underground, a Wilder hangout? How did those guys even get in?"

Pam shrugged. "It's a free country, like it or not. And lately I'm *not* liking it."

"Me either," George said, thinking about how unpleasant things seemed recently. Reva being mugged, now these racial slurs hurled at Jamal and Pam.

"Jamal and I have been hanging out a lot together since then," Pam said. "To tell you the truth, George, I'm kind of worried about Jamal. I mean, he was so angry at those guys—the situation could have gotten way out of control."

"Do you think he's looking for that guy or something?" George asked.

"No. But if he saw him again, I don't know what would happen," Pam said. "He's gotten even angrier since that night because we both keep thinking about the junk that skinhead said."

"Wow. It must be hard to concentrate on anything else," George said, standing up. "I'm *really* sorry, Pam."

Pam shrugged. "It's not your fault."

"I know. I just hate that it happened to you and Jamal," George said. She pulled the curtains on their window closed. "Sleep all you want. I'll be back in about an hour, okay?"

"Are you sure you should go by yourself? I heard about Reva getting mugged," Pam said, concerned.

"Who's going to mug me in broad daylight *and* looking like this?" George pointed at her black nylon running tights and her long Wilder T-shirt. "All I have on me is a key, and that's tied to my shoe. Anyway, I'll be going too fast for anyone to catch me."

Pam laughed. "Uh-huh. Well, be careful, Ms. Iron Woman."

George laughed. "I'm not about to do a triathlon. Anyway, I'll hardly be alone. Believe it or not, there are a couple of hundred people out there heading to an eight o'clock class right now," George said.

"Fools." Pam snuggled back under her comforter, pulling the covers up around her neck.

George laughed and unlocked the door. She headed downstairs and outside. Placing one palm on the brick wall of the dorm, George started her stretching routine, pulling her foot up behind her. She had just switched legs when somebody shoved her up against the wall.

"Hey!" she yelled as her head brushed the brick. "What are you doing?" Out of the corner of her eye she saw a piece of white paper tossed onto the ground beside her.

Then the pressure on her was suddenly gone. Whoever had trapped her had taken off just as fast. "Hey!" she cried, turning, her voice shaky with fear.

As George spun around, she thought she caught sight of a black jacket in the bushes along the side of Jamison—but that was it.

Whoever it was seemed to be tall and strong.

And gone, she realized, as she looked around the side of the building. There was nobody in sight.

What in the world was that all about? she

wondered, massaging the part of her thigh that had hit the wall. Had somebody tried to mug her, too?

George was about to go back inside and tell Pam what happened when she noticed the small piece of paper she'd seen tossed on the ground. She leaned over to pick it up.

She unfolded the paper, which had a typed note on it. In large capital letters, it said, "Send your Indian chief back to the reservation."

Stunned, George grasped the dorm door, then quickly opened the nylon pouch on her sneaker to get her dorm key. She had to call Will right away!

"Nancy! I'm so glad I caught you!" Bess exclaimed.

"Hi! Guess what? I'm on my way to meet Anna, my new little sister from Helping Hands," Nancy said, the door to Thayer closing softly behind her.

"I have to talk to you about something," Bess said.

"Okay, but I don't have much time," Nancy said, glancing at her watch. "I have to pick Anna up soon. What's up?"

Bess took a step closer to Nancy and put a hand on her arm. "It's about George. This morning she was attacked," Bess said. "Like Reva. Only—not like Reva."

"Wait—what do you mean? You're talking

in circles, Bess. Just tell me—was she hurt?" Nancy asked.

"No. She's fine," Bess said. "I just spoke with her on the phone, and she wasn't injured. George was about to go for her morning run, and as she was stretching, someone came up behind her and shoved her into the wall. But it might not be the same guy who mugged Reva. The guy didn't try to get any money and he also left George a horrible note."

"A note?" Nancy's nose wrinkled. "What are you talking about? What kind of note?"

"A really nasty, totally racist one," Bess said, slumping down on a bench outside the dorm. "It said something like 'Why don't you send your Indian chief boyfriend back to the reservation.' Can you believe someone would even *write* a note like that?"

"Frankly? Yes," Nancy said. "From what I've heard, there's a racist group here in Weston. But why would they—or anyone—care whom George dates? I mean, who's George to them? What's she ever done to get their attention?"

"Or Will, for that matter," Bess commented. She was silent for a minute before looking at Nancy. "Why would they write a note like that, anyway—much less push George in a threatening way just to deliver it?" she asked Nancy.

"Somebody who wanted to scare her away from Will or from dating him," Nancy replied.

"This racist group I've heard about believes in keeping ethnic groups separate. George is Caucasian and Will is Native American. She could have been targeted because of their relationship."

"Well, they picked the wrong person if they were looking to really scare anyone," Bess said with a small laugh, picturing her cousin. "Knowing George, and the way she feels about Will, that isn't going to work."

Nancy nodded. "True. So how *is* she doing? Should we go see her? Oh—I can't. I have to get Anna. Later, though."

"She's pretty upset," Bess said. "I'm going back to the dorm to see her now."

"Did she say she got a look at the person who pushed her?" Nancy asked.

"Not really. It all happened incredibly fast," Bess said. "Whoever it was shoved her into the wall and ran off after dropping the note. By the time she turned around, he was gone. There are all those bushes around Jamison, you know?"

"You said 'he'—is she sure it was a guy?" Nancy asked. "I mean, did he say anything to her?"

"No. I guess she assumed it was a guy because whoever it was was pretty big and strong. You mentioned some racist group—do you think it's the same person who went after Reva?"

46

"It could be," Nancy said thoughtfully. "Who knows? I can't imagine how their sick minds work."

"Oh! That reminds me! George told me that Pam and Jamal got into a big argument with some skinheads down at the Underground Tuesday night after they shouted some racist stuff at her and Jamal," Bess said. "What's going on around here lately?"

"I don't know," Nancy said. "All I know right now is that things are getting really weird and scary."

"I agree," Bess said. "Well—I'm going back to Jamison to see George."

"Can I drop you off on my way into town?" Nancy asked.

Bess laughed. "Sure, why walk when I can hitch a ride."

"Right," Nancy said. "Hey, thanks for coming over to tell me about George. Give her my love, okay?" She and Bess walked across the parking lot to Nancy's car.

"I'm not leaving her side!" Bess declared. Not after that disgusting note, she said to herself. Bess couldn't imagine getting a threat like that about somebody she was involved with. If anyone tried to keep her away from Paul— she'd flatten him.

I wonder what she's like, Nancy thought as she pressed the doorbell. Why do I feel so nervous? She's just a kid, Nancy reminded herself. There's nothing to worry about!

The counselor from Helping Hands had told Nancy that Anna's mother was dead and that she had no brothers or sisters. Her only family was her father, who worked long hours as a carpet and floor installer. A teacher at Anna's school had recommended her to Helping Hands, thinking she could use a Wilder big sister.

Most of the teenage kids who went to Helping Hands were there because they didn't have the traditional support networks they needed. They usually had no siblings and most came from single-parent families.

A thin, pretty girl with long blond hair opened the door and gazed nervously at Nancy. "Hi," she said shyly.

"Hi, are you Anna?"

The girl nodded slowly, biting her lip.

"I'm Nancy. It's nice to meet you," Nancy said.

"Um—you can come in, I guess," Anna said, stepping back a bit.

"Thanks." Anna led her into the kitchen, where they both sat at a table by the window.

"Do you want something to drink?" Anna offered.

"No, I'm fine. But, thanks," Nancy said. "So, what do you feel like doing today?"

Anna shrugged. "I don't know."

"Well—I have a car, so we have lots of options," Nancy said. "We could go for a drive or hang out at a coffee shop—I guess you probably don't drink coffee, though, huh?"

"Not usually," Anna said with a slight shrug. "My dad has it every morning, though. Like, religiously."

Nancy laughed. "My boyfriend's like that."

"You have a boyfriend?" Anna asked.

"Yes. His name's Jake. You'll get to meet him sometime, I hope." That is, if I ever find some time to see him, Nancy thought. "Do you have a boyfriend? Or someone you like at school?"

Anna shrugged, and her face turned a little pink. "No."

"So, what do you feel like doing?" Nancy asked again. "Not that we have to do anything—we could just hang out and talk if you want."

"No, I'd like to go somewhere," Anna said. "How about the mall? I just got my allowance."

Nancy grinned as she headed for the front door. "Let's go."

"This place looks like a club or something," Anna joked as she and Nancy walked into Major Attitude, a clothing store at the mall.

Nancy laughed. Anna was right—the place did look like a club. The entire store was decorated in stark black and white, with bright lights flashing over displays of the latest trendy clothes and loud hip-hop music blasting out of the speakers.

"See anything you like?" Nancy asked, as they paused in front of a rack marked New Arrivals.

"That is *so* cool." Anna started to pick up a black- and white-checked cropped jacket.

"I saw it first!" A hand reached out from the other side of the rack and snatched the jacket off the hanger.

Anna looked at Nancy. "Talk about a serious shopper."

Funny, Nancy thought. That voice sounded awfully familiar. "Kara?" she asked, peering around the other side of the rack.

"I think that's my roommate," Nancy explained to Anna. "She's a shopping addict."

"I heard that." Kara's face emerged through the top of a turtleneck sweater, as she pulled it off. She stared at Anna for a second. "Cool belt. Can I borrow it sometime?" she asked. "Wait a second—you're Anna, right?"

Anna nodded. "Hi. Now can I have that jacket back? I want to try it on." She held out her hand.

"Well, okay." Kara handed her the checkered jacket. "I guess I have enough here already." She started looking through a pile of sweaters and dividing them into groups. "This one I have to get, this one I could live without, have to get, live without—"

"Loves me, loves me not," Nancy interjected. She glanced at Anna, who was modeling the jacket in front of a three-way mirror. "Hey, I thought you and Tim were studying together this afternoon."

"We are," Kara said. "Just . . . a little later, that's all."

"Uh-huh." Nancy nodded knowingly. Kara always put her homework off until the last minute, and the fact that she and Tim Downing were dating now didn't help. "So, what do you think?" Nancy asked Anna as she came back over to them.

"I think I love it," Anna said. "And I also think it's a hundred and forty-nine dollars."

Kara grabbed the jacket from Anna and shoved it back onto the rack. "Don't get it now. Wait until it's in the Final Clearance section, back there." Kara pointed to a section behind them.

"Are you going to get anything?" Anna asked, looking at Kara.

"Do you think I should?" Kara asked.

"Like you'll listen to what we say," Nancy commented.

"What do you guys think of this one? Or this one?" Kara held up the sweaters in her have-to-get pile against her.

"I like that one." Anna pointed to the

brown one. "Maybe *I* can borrow it some-time." She looked at Kara and grinned.

"You know, it's amazing, but she's actually just like my little sister. How do you do that?" Kara asked, shaking her head.

Nancy laughed. "Hey, Anna and I were going to grab a snack. Do you want to hit the food court with us?" she asked Kara.

"I'd love to, but I'm supposed to meet Tim in half an hour, and I really can't decide be-tween this and—ooh, look at those! They'd go perfectly!" Kara hurried off in the direction of a new leggings display. "Nice meeting you, Anna—I'm sure I'll see you again!" Kara called over her shoulder.

"Don't study too hard!" Nancy called after her.

Kara turned around mid-stride and stuck out her tongue.

"Having a roommate must be fun," Anna commented when she and Nancy sat down in the food court with their sodas.

"It is," Nancy agreed. "Most of the time, anyway." She thought of all the times Kara had borrowed things of hers without asking. "Hey, I was thinking—maybe you and I should decide what we're going to do next week. I'll come over about the same time. Thursday af-ternoons are good for you, right?"

"Sure. But—" There was a note of disap-pointment in Anna's voice.

"But what?" Nancy asked. "Isn't this working out for you?"

"Oh, yeah—it's great!" Anna smiled at her. "I was just wondering, you know, if maybe we could do something before next week. Like, this weekend or whatever." Anna stirred her soda with the straw.

"This weekend? Well, okay," Nancy said. "Let me just think for a second and figure where I can find the time." She ran through the list of things she'd already planned. She wanted to see George. She had an article due; she was supposed to cover the arts and crafts show that Friday. She wanted to spend her Saturday night with Jake—if not all of it, at least part of it.

But Anna looked so eager that Nancy found it hard to say no to her.

"Okay, sure," Nancy said. "How about if we go to a movie Saturday night?"

"Great!" Anna cried, smiling.

Seeing her smile again, Nancy knew she'd done the right thing. Now, if only she could find a way to make Jake feel as happy about her breaking their dinner date.

Still, she was just going to a movie with Anna—and an early movie, at that. She and Jake would still have time to spend together.

But not enough!

CHAPTER 5

Jake slid into a seat at a crowded booth in the back of the Souvlaki House, a great all-hours diner that served the best Greek food in Weston.

"Hey, everyone, what's up?" he greeted the group.

Several members of the Animal Rescue League, which Jake had recently joined, were meeting for dinner on Thursday to discuss upcoming projects.

"Not much, Jake. How are you?" Mike asked.

"Pretty good. I'll be better after one of Stavros's major slabs of moussaka. I'm starving." Jake rubbed his stomach, which had growled the whole way through his late-afternoon class. He'd been counting the minutes to dinner for the past half hour.

"I'm getting the Greek salad," Chaz said.

Jake nodded. "Sounds good."

For a second he wondered what Nancy was doing for dinner. He wished he were sharing a table with her instead of his buddies in the Animal Rescue League. But there would be time for Nancy eventually.

"So what's new at the *Wilder Times*?" Sarah asked Jake. "Any late-breaking stories we should know about?"

"Sorry. You'll have to wait for the paper like everyone else," Jake said with a shrug.

"Hey, I heard about something I wanted to discuss," Amy said.

"What's that?" Sarah asked.

"There's this used car lot on the outskirts of town—Route Twelve, I think," Amy said. "Well, turns out the owner keeps some dogs there to protect his cars from getting ripped off. And the dogs are being completely mistreated." She shook her head. "A friend of mine told me about it, so I checked it out. There are a couple of dogs, and they are the skinniest I've ever seen—their ribs are showing and everything."

"The guy must be starving them to make them meaner, so they'll protect his property even more fiercely," Mike surmised.

Amy nodded. "Yeah. Exactly."

"Do you think he's really not feeding them?" Jake asked. "That's hard to believe."

"If the owner is feeding them, it's barely at all," Amy said. "And I think we should do something about it."

"Those definitely sound like dogs that need rescuing," Chaz agreed, nodding. "Let's plan a raid on the place."

"A raid?" another Animal League member asked. "Are you sure that's a good idea?"

"We have to get them. The most important thing is saving them before they starve to death," Amy said.

"We can probably find homes for all of them," Mike declared.

Jake felt uneasy. "They do belong to someone, though," he pointed out. "Do you think you should just try to take them like that? And what if you get bitten?"

"I agree with Jake. Maybe you shouldn't get so carried away before you look into this a little," another member said. "The guy might not know what he's doing. Or maybe he's poor—"

"The guy owns a business—he can afford to feed his dogs," Mike interrupted. "And I can't wait to tell him what a piece of scum he is!"

Jake had never heard Mike so angry before. He was very passionate about animal rights, sometimes so much so that it worried Jake, like now. Rescuing stray animals from the street was one thing, but breaking into private property and stealing dogs seemed a little too passionate to Jake.

Nancy couldn't believe how tired she felt. The only thing she'd done was hang out with Anna, shopping and talking. But, she knew, she couldn't be tired; she had to work on two different papers that night.

Time for a double cappuccino, she thought. Maybe I should go over to Java Joe's to study. As she opened the door to Thayer, she almost crashed into Dawn, who was on her way out of the dorm.

"Whoa!" Dawn cried, taking a step backward. "Sorry, Nance."

"In a hurry much?" Nancy teased, lightly punching Dawn on the arm.

"I guess I was thinking about other things," Dawn said. "I'm on my way to the dean's office."

"Uh-oh. That can't be good news, can it?" Nancy suddenly realized that Dawn looked upset.

"No, it's not good," Dawn said slowly. "Nancy, some really frightening things are happening around here, and I'm very worried."

"Is this about what happened to Reva? Or is there something else you're seeing the dean about?" Nancy asked, growing more concerned.

"A student on the fourth floor had his motorcycle vandalized last night," Dawn answered. "And that added on top of Reva's being mugged, I just feel that Thayer's not as safe as we thought it was."

"To tell you the truth, I've been kind of worried, too," Nancy said. "Come on, let's go inside and talk." As they walked back into Thayer, Nancy thought about what had happened to George that morning. Will was Native American, Reva was African American. . . . Was there a connection with the CWP? "Dawn," she asked, "do you know the guy whose motorcycle was vandalized?"

"Sure," Dawn said with a shrug. "Why?"

"Well—this might sound really strange. But is he Caucasian?" Nancy asked.

"No. He's Vietnamese," Dawn said. "Why did you want to know that?" Her forehead was creased with concern.

Dawn followed Nancy over to the far corner of the dorm's lobby, and they perched on the window ledge.

"First there was the attack on Reva, right?" Nancy said. "And she's African American. That was Tuesday night."

Dawn nodded. "Right."

"And I found out that another incident happened to my friend George," Nancy said.

"You're kidding! Her, too? Is she all right?" Dawn asked.

"She's fine. I mean, as fine as she could be,

considering she's been threatened." Nancy quickly explained the note that had been thrown at George's feet early that morning. "And George's roommate, Pam, told her that some skinheads harassed Pam and her boyfriend, Jamal, on Tuesday night at the Underground, insulting them because they're African American."

"So all of a sudden a lot of stuff is happening," Dawn said, tracing a circle on the windowpane. "And it all seems related to race. How awful. What's happening around here?"

"I'm not sure," Nancy said. "All these things do seem race related." She decided to tell Dawn about the Citizens for White Purity organization. "There's a group on campus that believes the races should be separate. I can't help thinking they're responsible for all this."

"What group?" Dawn asked.

"Citizens for White Purity," Nancy said.

"Ugh," Dawn groaned. "Catchy name."

"I know. Their headquarters are here in Weston somewhere, but lately they've been on campus to recruit students. Jake is investigating them for a story," Nancy explained. "I feel like helping him, the way things are going."

"Maybe you guys will find out something that connects these incidents to that group," Dawn said hopefully. "Campus security is looking into the attacks, so with any luck, this is the last time we have to discuss this."

Nancy shrugged. "I hope so."

"Now, how about I meet you at Java Joe's," Dawn said. "Order me a café mocha at about—six-fifteen, okay?"

Nancy laughed. "You want it to be ready when you get there?"

"On second thought, meeting with the dean always has this incredibly tiring effect on me," Dawn mused, standing up. "Better make it a double espresso."

"I'll see you there in half an hour," Nancy said. "I'll be at the table with all the cups!"

"Okay. Okay. 'Today's American Family,' " Kara read from her class assignment sheet as she sat on her bed next to Tim.

"You've said that about eight times already!" Tim laughed.

"Oh, yeah? And I'm going to keep on saying it, until *you* come up with an idea for our project!" Kara gave Tim a stern look, then she dissolved into laughter, too.

She and Tim were supposed to be spending the evening working on their psychology class project. But Kara always had so much fun with Tim that she was finding it impossible to concentrate and take the assignment seriously. It was due soon, and they'd have to work fast to get it done, so they had to start it that night.

"Okay," she began again. " 'Today's Amer—' "

"No!" Tim cried, putting his hand over Kara's mouth. "Don't say it!"

Suddenly the door swung open and Nancy walked into the room. She took one look at the two of them and said, "Studying hard as usual, I see."

Kara laughed, prying Tim's hand off her mouth. "I was *trying* to. Only Tim here isn't helping much."

"Oh, like you're coming up with so many great ideas?" Tim retorted. "The last idea you had was to get sodas for us."

"Hey. At least when I have an idea, it's a *good* one," Kara said.

"True." Tim nodded and clinked his soda can against Kara's knee before taking a drink of his root beer.

"What are you guys working on—or at least what are you supposed to be working on?" Nancy asked. She set her backpack on the floor and sat on her bed.

"We have to do this report about 'Today's American Family,'" Tim said. "We're supposed to pick an aspect of family life to study, do some surveys, gather information, and write it all up."

"By next Friday." Kara grinned. "Boy, do I love college."

"Deadlines are fun, aren't they?" Nancy replied. "I have a few of my own this week. You know, I think all the professors think that we have only one class—theirs."

"Exactly." Kara looked at Nancy. "Come on, help us, *please*. Come up with an idea!"

Kara waited as Nancy thought for a minute. "Okay, here's an idea," Nancy said. "Why don't you do your report on American families who procrastinate?"

Tim laughed. "But they'd never fill out the surveys!"

"Come on, you guys. Be serious," Kara urged.

"Sorry—I'm out of ideas," Nancy said, standing up. "And I have to call George, and then I'm meeting Dawn," she said. "Since you guys are so busy *studying,* I'm going to use the lounge phone. Good luck!"

"Wait! Nancy!" Kara cried as her roommate closed the door. She sank back onto her pillow, feeling utterly defeated. "Now what are we going to do?"

"Gee, thanks for the vote of confidence," Tim said, frowning. "Don't worry, we'll come up with something."

"I guess you're right," Kara said. But she *was* starting to worry. What if they really couldn't come up with anything original? The last thing she needed was a low grade in psych!

"Charley, I'm *really* sorry about yesterday," Casey said. She was perched on the edge of her bed, enjoying the rare moment of privacy she'd have until Stephanie got back from the library. "I felt awful about our conversation ending on such a lousy note."

"So did I," Charley said, his voice more subdued than usual.

"It's just that I didn't have any privacy—I was sitting in the middle of the lounge with people coming in and out. I mean, this is too serious to talk about on the phone to begin with, and then, not to be alone when we're talking . . . it was murder!" Casey said. She hoped Charley would understand.

"So are you in your room now?" Charley asked.

"Yes. All alone—I love it," Casey said. "Not that it'll last. Stephanie's coming home as soon as she gets the books she needs from the library."

"Then we'd better make it fast," Charley said.

"Make what fast? Our conversation?" Casey asked.

"Your answer. Yes or no," Charley urged. "Will you marry me, Casey? And please don't make me ask again—it was hard enough the first time."

Casey tugged at a loose strand on the throw rug in her room. "Charley, I still don't know," she said.

"What?" he practically cried. "How can you still *not know?*"

"Because! As I told you before, it's a huge decision," Casey said. "It's not just marrying you, which I'd be thrilled to do. You want me to leave school and move back to California. That's like two different decisions."

"So what are you saying? You'll only marry me if I move there?" Charley scoffed. "I have my whole career going here, in case you've forgotten."

"No, of course I haven't forgotten, and no, I'm not expecting you to move here for me," Casey said. "But that's what you're expecting from me. And as much as I love you—"

"Are you sure?" Charley interjected.

"Charley, how many times can I tell you? I love you I love you I love you," Casey declared.

There was silence on the other end for a minute. Casey didn't know what to say next.

"If you really loved me, you'd say yes right away without dragging it out," Charley finally said in a quiet voice. "If you don't want to marry me, just get up the nerve to say so. And if you do, I'll be waiting to hear from you. 'Bye, Case."

"But, Charley—" Casey began to protest. Then she realized the line was dead. Charley had hung up, just like the other day. He was angry, hurt, and upset with her.

Casey supposed he had a right to be; but didn't she have a right to make a decision in her own time? If she rushed things, it wouldn't be good for either of them.

Maybe I ought to just flip a coin, she thought, feeling dejected. It would be a lot easier than lying awake at night, wondering and worrying about what to do.

She collapsed on top of her bed and stared at the ceiling. She thought of how it felt when Charley had his arms around her and how wonderfully sweet and passionate his kisses could be. Why was deciding to marry him so difficult?

CHAPTER 6

Stephanie stood at the window of her dorm room, drumming her manicured fingernails against the window ledge. It was Friday morning, and her father, R. J. Keats, was already twenty minutes late—and he was never late for anything, ever. It had to be the influence of his new wife, Kirsten—Kiki—Stephanie decided with a frown.

Stephanie had never met Kiki, and she was dreading the weekend even more than final exam week. She loved her father dearly and only wanted him to be happy.

But was a new wife who was only twenty-eight—nearly half his age—going to make him happy? Stephanie sincerely doubted it. Anyway, she and her dad had gotten along fine on their own for years. Why did he have to get remarried? It changed everything.

Now when her father called, it was "Kiki this" and "Kiki that." The fact that he had a nickname for her was sickening enough by itself, but then he wouldn't stop talking about her. Whenever Stephanie tried to talk about her life or tell her father what was going on at Wilder, her father didn't seem interested. He was so crazy about Kirsten that they'd gotten married without Stephanie's even being there.

As much as Stephanie was dreading this weekend, though, she'd made up her mind to use it to her advantage. If her father thought she was going to sit there and be nice, he was wrong. Stephanie was going to remind him who was the most important person in his life—his daughter.

Of course, having them visit was a major plus in the "goodies" department. Stephanie was looking forward to fancy meals and a shopping spree or two. She could get along with Kiki just fine, as long as the "stuff" kept coming.

As her bedroom door was opened, Stephanie turned around to watch Casey walk into the room. "Hey, Steph. Any sign of your parents yet?"

"It's my father and his new wife," Stephanie corrected her. "What's with you, anyway?"

"I'm depressed," Casey said.

"Oh." Stephanie peered out at the parking

lot. Even though she'd seen pictures of Kiki, she couldn't imagine her getting out of her father's car and walking up to Thayer with him. As if they *belonged* together. "Well, that makes two of us. Can you believe I have to hang out with my father and Kiki all weekend?"

"Kiki. That's some nickname," Casey agreed.

Stephanie frowned. "Tell me about it. Does any self-respecting woman over the age of ten allow herself to be called Kiki when her name is Kirsten? That would be like me calling myself Steph-Steph."

Casey laughed wryly. "Please don't."

"Why do people have to get married so fast anyway?" Stephanie complained. "He could have dated her for at least a year. What's the big rush, anyway?"

"I don't know. They're in love, aren't they?" Casey asked. She looked very intense all of a sudden.

"He *says* they are," Stephanie grumbled.

"So why shouldn't they get married?" Casey asked.

"Because! It's totally tacky, that's why. She's half his age. I can't believe you would sit here and try to argue the point with me! I need a cigarette." Stephanie grabbed her pack of cigarettes and lighter off her dresser. "I'll be in the lounge if my dad calls to say he's canceling our weekend because his precious Kiki's carsick."

Stephanie hurried to the lounge. It was a relief to get out of her room. She could hardly believe Casey's nerve, suggesting that it was okay for her father to remarry someone as young as Kiki.

"Hey! Stephanie!" Kara was headed into the suite just as Stephanie walked toward the lounge. "How's it going?"

"Rotten." Stephanie slipped a cigarette out of the pack and lit it, taking a long drag.

"You seem kind of—anxious," Kara commented. "Is everything okay?"

"I'm not anxious," Stephanie muttered.

"Really? You seem wound up about something," Kara said.

Wound up? How about *fed* up, Stephanie thought. "Well, how would you feel if you had to entertain your new twenty-eight-year-old stepmother all weekend?" Stephanie demanded.

"Pretty anxious, I guess," Kara admitted. "What's she like?"

"Who cares what she's like—she's ruining my life!" Stephanie took another drag of her cigarette. "*Anxious* is not the word. *Furious*, maybe."

"That's too bad," Kara said. "I mean, I'm sorry you have to spend your weekend playing hostess to someone you don't like."

"Like her. I've never even *met* her!" Stephanie cried.

Kara's eyes widened. "You know what? I just thought of something. Maybe you could help me later."

"With what? I don't have any extra time—"

"It won't take long. Anyway, you're busy now—I'll get back to you, okay!" Kara went down the hall to her room.

Stephanie shrugged. "Whatever." She swore she'd never understand Kara or half the girls in her suite. Casey—what did she have to be depressed about? She only had the most gorgeous, wonderful boyfriend in the whole world, not to mention an acting career she could go back to anytime she wanted, and enough money from her television show to live on for the next few years.

Some people were never satisfied, Stephanie thought, dropping her cigarette in someone's cup of cold coffee.

Nancy stopped in front of a painting in the Kaplan Arts Center. She cocked her head to the left, then turned it to the right. She couldn't make sense of the wildly swirled lines. But maybe that was the point, she decided.

She surveyed the room, making a few notes on the legal pad she was carrying. The Arts Center's noon reception for the opening of the World Arts & Crafts Show was drawing a fairly large crowd. Since Kaplan was close to the Student Union, a lot of students had stopped by on their way to and from lunch and the bookstore.

Nancy moved on slowly, trying to jot down quick descriptions of the variety of exhibits. She stopped in front of a table where various bright, multicolored fabrics were displayed. Beside the fabrics were wooden sculptures.

"Look at those colors," a woman behind Nancy said.

"That's really cool," her friend agreed. "How did you make that?"

One of the artists standing behind the table stepped forward. "Actually, it's an old African tradition. The dyes are made using all-natural substances. Here—this explains the process." He handed a sheet of paper to the student.

Nancy smiled at him. "They're really beautiful. Did you make these, too?" She gestured to the wooden sculptures.

"No, she did." He pointed to a woman beside him.

"That must take a long time," Nancy said, picking up one of the sculptures to examine it more closely.

"Yeah. But it's fun, too," she said.

"Does this have any special meaning or significance to you?" Nancy asked. "In other words, how did you come up with this shape in particular?"

"Well, I went to Africa for a semester abroad to study art...." The woman talked to Nancy for a few minutes, giving her some background on her work, before Nancy moved on to another exhibit.

"Yo, Jack! Check this out!" Nancy looked up as she heard a loud yell.

Standing in front of the table with the fabric and wooden sculptures was a tall, burly guy wearing a sleeveless denim shirt. His head was shaved to a buzz cut, and he wore motorcycle boots and a large metal key chain dangling from one pocket.

"What's all this junk?" he asked gruffly, pointing at one of the sculptures.

"And what's it doing here?" The friend whom he'd called out to, a tall guy also dressed in jeans and heavy boots, walked over to the table.

"It's African art," one of the artists said stiffly.

"African art? Isn't that a contradiction in terms?" The burly skinhead laughed.

As Nancy listened to them, she felt like punching this guy. Why was he being such a jerk?

"It's a waste of space, and I don't think it should be here," one of the skinheads said.

"Why don't you guys just keep going?" the woman artist suggested.

"It's junk," the tall guy said, standing right

in front of the table. "And I don't think it deserves the table it's sitting on."

"Right on, Wayne," the other skinhead agreed.

Wayne, Nancy thought. Where had she heard that name before?

"This isn't art, it's ignorant trash," he continued, his voice becoming louder and louder. "You know what I think of your stupid tribal totems and masks?" He picked one up off the table.

"Hey—put that down," the woman said. "If you don't like it, just get out of here."

"Me? I should get out of here?" He chuckled. "Oh, that's a good one. I should leave. Look, babe, I'm an American. A white, red-blooded full citizen of the United States of America. I'm not going anywhere. But maybe you and your so-called art should!" He lifted up a mask and brought it down on his knee, smashing the carefully carved piece in half.

"Hey!" the woman cried, practically jumping over the table to stop him from wrecking anything else.

But she was too late. Wayne overturned the table, throwing everything onto the floor, then he ran over to another table, where an artist was exhibiting Asian art. With one sweep of his arm, Wayne dumped several ceramic items onto the floor.

Wayne, Nancy suddenly realized. This must

be Wayne French, the leader of Citizens for White Purity that Jake had told her about.

The sound of breaking glass brought the security guard who'd been posted over at the doorway running. "Stop right now!" the guard demanded, grabbing Wayne's arm.

Were Wayne French and his group behind all the crime that had happened lately on campus? Nancy wondered as she watched backup security guards arrive to hustle away his friends.

"I'm really sorry," Nancy told the woman whose mask had been destroyed. "That guy was totally out of line."

The artist was too distraught to answer as she slowly picked up pieces of her mask.

"You're a pig, you know that!" somebody shouted at Wayne as the guard led him, handcuffed, to the door.

"The anger is rising, people!" Wayne shouted in reply. "This is just the beginning!"

"Wrong, pal. You're going to jail! This is the end!" a woman screamed back.

"There are others who will take my place! And more acts of violence will occur as long as the races try to mix! The white race is pure and should not be contaminated! This is our country!"

Wayne's final shouts were drowned out as he was escorted from the building.

Nancy felt sick to her stomach. She'd never

heard such violent, hateful statements uttered out loud before—at least, not in her presence. And from what she'd seen, Wayne obviously had followers who believed in him. If the Citizens for White Purity group wasn't stopped, they'd probably carry out even more violent acts—against anyone who wasn't white.

Bess felt like whistling as she strolled across campus to the Kappa house. Whistling . . . or dancing. She loved Friday afternoons more than anything. It was a great feeling to know you were done with your classes for the week, but you weren't expected to start your weekend homework yet.

Bess practically lived for weekends. She had been trying to cut down on her partying so she could stay on at Wilder for the next four years and graduate.

When she got closer to the Kappa house, she saw something she couldn't believe. A car was actually parked on the front porch, blocking the front door! "What the . . ." she muttered, walking up the sidewalk.

She recognized the small blue hatchback instantly, with the vanity license plates that said HOLLEE. The car belonged to Holly Thornton, the Kappa vice president. Holly was the one who had encouraged Bess to pledge Kappa in the first place, and they'd since become good friends.

I never knew Holly was so bad at parking, Bess thought with a smile as she walked around to the back of the house and went up the stairs that led into the kitchen.

"Well, I don't know how it got there, but it was there when I woke up this morning," Holly was saying when Bess walked into the giant living room. "And I know I didn't drive it there."

"You didn't lend it to anyone? Like ... the worst driver in the house?" Eileen asked.

"Hi, you guys!" Bess said, grabbing a seat next to them. "Holly! Did you ever take drivers' ed, or didn't they have that at your high school?"

Holly laughed. "Hey, I might have flunked the three-point turn, but I know how to park, okay? And that is not my work."

"Then who borrowed your car?" Eileen asked.

"I don't think anyone borrowed it, someone moved it up there. Here, look at this." Holly held a piece of yellow lined paper out to Bess and Eileen.

Bess took the note and read it. "Care to *gamble* on who we are?" it said in block script. Bess didn't recognize the handwriting. " 'We,' " she said out loud. "That means ... wait a second! They underlined the word *gamble*."

"Yeah, we saw that," Eileen said. "And your point would be . . . ?"

"Don't you guys remember?" Bess couldn't believe the guys in Paul's fraternity would actually pull off something like this. So much for accusing them of being all talk and no action!

"Remember what?" Holly looked confused.

"At the Black and White Nights party," Bess explained, referring to a big fund-raising event held the week before. "We made that side bet with the Zeta guys about who would raise the most money that night. Well, we won. So now *they're* trying to get back at us."

Eileen nodded. "Works for me."

"It's the only thing that makes sense," Holly agreed.

Bess picked up the phone from the wall. "I'll call Paul and find out if Zeta's behind this little stunt," she offered.

She dialed her boyfriend Paul's number at the Zeta house. After two rings, he answered the phone.

"So what's the idea of leaving a car on the porch?" Bess asked before Paul could even finish saying hello. "Is that supposed to be funny or something?"

"Um . . . Bess? What are you talking about?" Paul replied after a few seconds.

"You know. You decided to get back at us for winning more money by putting a car on our porch, which by the way is totally blocking *everything*," Bess went on in a teasing voice.

"Really? There's a car on your porch?" Paul asked. "What color? Is it for sale?"

"No, it's not for sale. It's Holly's car—as if you don't know that it's blue!" Bess shook her head, laughing. Then she put on her best conspiratorial voice. "Come on, Paul. You can tell *me*. How did you guys get it up there, anyway?" She was hoping the last question would trick Paul into telling the truth.

"Bess, have you ever seen me lift a car before?" Paul asked.

"Well, no, but—"

"But nothing. I didn't do it, I'm telling you," Paul said.

"Not by yourself, but I'm sure you could have with your friends," Bess prompted. "Of course, if you don't want to tell me, that's fine. It's just that I thought honesty was important in our relationship, and I'd hate for us to start keeping secrets from each other." She looked at Holly and Eileen and winked.

"Look, Bess—I'm being completely honest! Honest! I have a lot of homework to do." There was a muffled snicker of laughter. "So are we still on for tonight?" Paul asked.

"I don't know. I guess it depends on

whether or not I can get out the front door over here," Bess said. "We'll see." She hung up the phone with a defiant click.

"So did you find out anything?" Holly asked.

Bess shook her head. "But he did sound like he was about to crack up laughing. It has to be the Zeta guys. I'm sure they decided to get back at us for winning the bet by upping the ante. Now we're up to major pranks. And guess what that means, guys?" Bess looked at Eileen. "It's our turn now. We have to think of the ultimate revenge plan."

"Okay, but while we're planning this little war with the Zetas, my car is still on the porch," Holly pointed out. "How are we going to get it off?"

"The way I see it, there are a couple of options," Bess said, glancing out the window. "One, build a ramp and drive it off."

"Build a ramp? Like we know how!" Eileen said. "I'm not exactly majoring in engineering, you know."

"Okay, then . . . if the Zeta guys put it there, they had to have carried it," Bess surmised. "And if they could carry it up, somebody could carry it down."

Eileen rolled her eyes. "Yeah, if Superman actually existed, maybe."

"We can't get Superman, that's true," Bess

agreed. "But maybe we could find ten guys who'll do it for us."

"And these ten guys would be where?" Holly asked.

"I'll find them," Bess said, and grinned at Holly. "Searching for hunks is a tough job, but hey, anything for Kappa!"

CHAPTER 7

Jake? Jake, are you here?" Nancy walked through the *Wilder Times* office, looking in every corner and cubicle. That's funny, she thought. He was usually in the office on Friday afternoons finishing up a piece, or a headline, or a caption.

"Don't tell me he actually got done *early*," she muttered, heading for the door.

"Nance!" Jake cried, rushing out of the copy room down the hall.

"Hi." Nancy smiled as he came toward her. "So where were you? Catching up on your photocopying?"

"Trying to. Until the dumb thing jammed again." Jake held up an ink-stained hand. "I was so busy trying to fix it, I didn't hear you come in." He put his arms around Nancy, being careful not to let his ink-stained hand touch her.

"Did you get it to work?" Nancy asked.

"Not exactly. Anyway, where have you been?" Jake gingerly brushed a strand of hair off Nancy's cheek. "What's going on?"

Nancy shook her head, loosening herself from Jake's arms. "What *isn't* going on."

Jake followed her over to the plate glass window overlooking the Wilder campus. "What do you mean?"

"There's so much happening right now, it's kind of overwhelming," Nancy said. "First Reva being mugged, and then—"

"There's more?" Jake asked.

"A lot more," Nancy said. "On Thursday morning somebody shoved George against her dorm wall as she was about to go for a run and left her a charming note about how she ought to drop her 'Indian chief' boyfriend."

"Seriously? That stinks." Jake put his hand on Nancy's back and rubbed gently.

"I agree," Nancy said. "And after that, I found out that this Vietnamese guy in Thayer had his motorcycle defaced with white paint. And then, worst of all, I just went to the World Arts and Crafts Show—you know, for my article?" Nancy turned to face Jake. "That Wayne guy was there with some other CWP members. At least, I'm pretty sure it was him. And they completely trashed a bunch of the art because it was African or Asian or—whatever!" She shook her head. "When the security guards came to drag him and his buddies off, he started shouting something about how the races shouldn't mix. Which means ..."

"George and Will," Jake guessed. "For example."

Nancy nodded. "I wouldn't be surprised at all if that jerk's behind what happened to George. As a matter of fact, I'll bet Wayne's responsible for all of it. After seeing what a mean and violent person he was."

Jake nodded. "It's only a matter of time before he and his group strikes again. Don't you think?" he asked.

"That's what scares me," Nancy confessed.

Jake reached out and took Nancy's hand. "Don't let this racist creep get to you. He's garbage!"

"I know he is. But if it is him and his sick group, they're hurting my friends," Nancy said.

"Okay," Jake said. "Let's think this through. If we believe CWP is behind all of these attacks, then it's going to be pretty hard for us to figure out exactly who's responsible for each one," Jake reasoned. "And even harder to come up with any real proof."

"Maybe. And I know it's not my job, but I just hate sitting around and waiting to hear about the *next* attack," Nancy said. She had a feeling Wayne's group might have something bigger in mind—some kind of statement.

"Look, if campus security came to kick out Wayne French and his pals today, they're going to be on the lookout for him and anyone who was with him," Jake said. "The CWP won't even be able to come onto campus anymore. Which means they can't do much."

Nancy shrugged slightly. Maybe Jake was right.

"Nancy, I know you want to help. So do I, believe me. What if we go ahead and pursue the article on them this weekend? Did I tell you that I found out where Wayne works—at an auto body shop in Weston? We can both pay him a visit, if you want. Assuming he's not in jail."

"Wouldn't that be great." Nancy stared at a calendar on the wall. "Okay, maybe we should visit him."

"Look, before we do anything else, let's have dinner together," Jake said. "We can talk about this, if you want, or we can forget about it completely and talk about you, or me, or— world peace. Whatever. *Please.* I'm starting to become a regular on the pizza delivery route."

Nancy smiled weakly, knowing Jake was only trying to cheer her up. "I'd love to have dinner with you, but I can't. I have too much to do tonight."

"Really? But it's Friday night," Jake argued.

"I know," Nancy said. "But I haven't had a chance to see George yet, and I've really got to do that. Plus, I need to write my article about what happened at the arts and crafts show.

"Oh. You know, if you could come up with worse reasons, I might have an argument here. But seeing George is important," Jake said. "Okay, so tonight's out, but let's make a plan for tomorrow night. Hey, we never checked out that jazz club over in Stoughton. Or we could go to the Underground."

Nancy shook her head. Why had she agreed to go to the movies with Anna when all she really wanted was to spend time with Jake? She felt like kicking herself!

"Can't do that, either?" Jake asked.

"No. You remember my little sister, Anna? Well, she asked about going to a movie, and I couldn't say no," Nancy told him. "I'm just getting to know her, and she's really lonely and all. I'm sorry."

"Me, too," Jake said, nodding.

Nancy looked into his eyes. "I'll make it up to you. I promise."

"Okay. Well, you'd better go catch George. Let me know how she's doing."

"I will. And thanks for being so understanding." Nancy kissed Jake goodbye. He wrapped his arms around her waist and pulled her closer, returning the kiss. Nancy couldn't believe she was passing up a weekend with Jake for any reason, however good it was. "Maybe I could meet you *after* the movie," she suddenly suggested.

"Wouldn't that be too late?" Jake asked.

"Too late for what?" Nancy replied, snuggling closer to him. "Midnight walks can be very romantic."

Jake ran his fingers through her hair. "I see your point. What time did you say that movie would be over again?"

"I'll call you," Nancy promised.

"Why don't you introduce Kiki to your friends, Stephanie? I'm sure she'd love to meet all of them," R. J. Keats said. He was wearing an expensive blue cashmere sweater that set off his deep blue eyes perfectly and complemented his graying hair. In Stephanie's opinion, R. J. was the very definition of distinguished.

Except when he was around Kiki. Then he turned into a babbling idiot, from what she'd observed so far.

Stephanie let out a deep sigh. Who cared whether Kiki wanted to meet her friends? What about what *she* wanted—which was to get to the restaurant as soon as possible.

Stephanie looked around the lounge. "Eileen? Kara? Casey? Dawn? This is Kiki," she said sweetly. "My father's new wife."

"And your stepmother, don't forget," R. J. Keats said.

How could I, Stephanie thought, glaring at Kiki.

Kiki flashed a bright smile at everyone. "It's so nice to meet you. I was hoping we'd get to know some of Stephanie's friends this weekend. So, you all share this one area?"

Stephanie nodded. "It's great." Except for the fact that somebody else was always in the space, that was.

Kiki put her expensive black leather purse down on the coffee table. "Of course, like all dorms, this one could use a little redecorating."

And you should know, Stephanie thought, glaring at her back, since you only *graduated* a couple of years ago. She was so young, it was ridiculous! Her dad was at least fifteen years older than Kiki. "Maybe you have some ideas you could give us," she said to Kiki. "Since you're such an expert in interior design."

"Oh, sure. I'd love to," Kiki replied, completely missing Stephanie's sarcasm.

"Kiki's redone our whole house," R. J. added. "And it looks wonderful. I can't wait for you to see it, Steph."

"Neither can I," Stephanie said. "So, where are we going for dinner?"

"I had heard Les Peches was nice," R. J. said.

"I love the food there," Stephanie interrupted. At least they'd be going to her favorite restaurant, so the night wouldn't be a total waste. "Great—I'll just grab my purse."

"But Kiki saw a place on the way into town that looked very interesting, so we thought we'd give it a try instead," R. J. finished.

"Did you," Stephanie said bitterly.

"It's called the Souvlaki House, I think," Kiki said.

"Souvlaki House? You want to go to *Souvlaki House?*" Stephanie couldn't believe it. Even though Stephanie loved Greek food, she could eat at Souvlaki House anytime—for under five bucks. She wanted something more extravagant. What was the point of parents visiting if they didn't take you somewhere good? "But it's not your kind of place, Dad. They don't take reservations, there's always a ton of college kids there, talking really loud, and there's a jukebox—I mean, it's essentially a *diner.*"

"Oh, Kiki and I are always up for an adventure," R. J. said, putting his arm around Kiki's waist. "Aren't we?"

"Definitely," she said, grinning at him.

Some adventure, Stephanie thought, glaring at her. More like a nightmare! Couldn't she even go to her favorite restaurant anymore?

And since when did her father like hanging out at diners?

His dumb midlife crisis was turning her life into a joke!

"Okay, but I hope you brought your antacid tablets," Stephanie muttered, heading for the door.

Or rather, she hoped they hadn't. For suggesting they eat at Souvlaki House, Kiki deserved whatever heartburn she got.

Jake walked out of the gym, his hair wet from the shower. There was nothing like a tough, hour-long workout to get out his frustration. Works every time, he thought, sauntering down the gym steps.

"Chaz, where are you off to?" he called to his friend from the Animal Rescue League, who was running past.

"Oh, hey, Jake," Chaz replied, waiting at the bottom of the steps for him. "How's it going?"

"Not great. Anyway, where are you off to in such a hurry?"

"I have to meet Mike," Chaz said.

Jake nodded. "What's up?"

"Another stray animal save," Chaz said. "Mike's at that convenience store downtown on Monroe Street. He found this litter of puppies behind the store. The mother had been hit by a car and killed."

"So what are you going to do?" Jake asked.

"Go get them," Chaz said. "I know a girl who's going to take care of the litter for a month while we find homes for them. Anyway, I'd better go—I have to meet Mike there in ten minutes. Oh, in case I didn't mention it yesterday, Mike's having a party tomorrow night. Two-twelve Dayton Street. You ought to come. Bring your girlfriend!" Chaz ran off down the sidewalk.

Jake thought about the invitation. He'd like to bring Nancy to the party. But she was already booked for Saturday night, and her plans didn't include him—at least not until after the night was almost over.

So he'd just go by himself.

"See what I was talking about?" Reva pointed to her computer screen. "Every time it's supposed to boot up, it gets stuck at this one part. It's not reading the hard drive."

"That's not good," Andy commented.

Reva laughed. "I know that! I asked you to come over so you could fix it, silly—not agree with me that it's hopelessly broken."

"Oh, and that's the only reason you called me? Well!" Andy stood up, flinging his burgundy wool scarf around his neck. "I see I'm not needed!"

"Basically—no, you're not," Reva said.

"Oh, is that how it is? Uh-huh." Andy nodded. "And I suppose you won't need me later tonight, when you get lonely and you start thinking about your incredibly gorgeous boyfriend who you pushed out into the cold, dark night."

"Nope, Probably not," Reva teased, shrugging.

"And you wouldn't miss this, either?" Andy reached out to Reva and tickled her waist.

Reva giggled. "No! Stop!" She leaped out of her chair and ran around the room, trying to escape Andy's tickling. He grabbed her arm and pulled her toward him.

They fell onto her bed, laughing.

Andy smothered Reva's neck with kisses. "Your computer is totally broken again. You need a new one. You realize that, don't you?"

Reva sighed. "You're so romantic."

"You'd better call that Darrell guy. He could probably fix it," Andy suggested.

Darrell, Reva thought. She still hadn't returned the gift he'd given her. But he hadn't been over to see her since then, so maybe he did understand she only wanted his friendship.

"Yes, I know. Actually, I left a couple of messages for Darrell, but he hasn't called back yet," Reva told Andy. "It's weird, because I think he has to have a beeper to work for Campus Computers. Doesn't he?"

Andy shrugged. "I don't remember. But

since it is Friday night, and your computer is busted, why don't we take advantage of it?"

"Meaning?" Reva asked.

"What do you think I mean?" Andy said, scooting closer to her. "Here we are, all alone . . . with nobody to bug us, no homework we can possibly do—"

"Say no more." Reva put her finger on Andy's lips. "I think I know exactly what you have in mind."

CHAPTER 8

"So tell me what happened." Nancy perched on the edge of George's bed and stared anxiously at her friend. George was doing her best to hide it, but Nancy could tell that she was still upset.

George fiddled with a pen on her desk. "As I told you on the phone, it happened so fast. I was stretching, then all of a sudden some guy shoved me into the brick wall. I scraped my head, and I was so stunned, I couldn't fight back or do anything. When I heard him run off, I turned around, and there was this piece of paper on the ground."

Nancy studied the note in her hand. She still couldn't get over how hateful it sounded. Why would anyone care that George was dating Will? Why did the CWP care about Will, period? And how did they even know who he was?

Unless they made it a point to search out all the nonwhites at Wilder every year, Nancy thought with a shudder. "So you don't remember anything else?" she asked George. "How big he was, or whether he had on any kind of aftershave, or what type of shoes he was wearing? Sorry—I sound like a police detective. I really don't mean to grill you. I just thought— maybe there's some little detail you remember."

"I didn't see anything," George said, shaking her head. "Except I thought I saw a dark jacket in the bushes. It lasted like—five seconds."

"But what a rotten five seconds, huh?" Nancy commented.

George nodded. "Yeah. I can't quite get over it. I mean, I can't stop worrying about who has something against Will and what they're going to do about it next."

"Me, too. Actually, I kind of have an idea of who might be behind it all, but it's too soon to know for sure," Nancy said. "What can you tell me about the argument Pam and Jamal got into at the Underground? Bess mentioned that a couple of skinheads were giving them a hard time."

"I guess they were on their way out when this guy started yelling at them about how they shouldn't be allowed in a public place like that," George said with a frown. "And he said something about how it was supposed to be for white people, or something like that. A real nut case, in other words."

That sounded exactly like Wayne French talking, Nancy thought. The language was the same as in the Citizens for White Purity pamphlet she'd read.

"So who do you think it is?" George asked.

"Well, I can't be a hundred percent sure," Nancy said. "But there's a group that's been on campus lately, and it sounds like their style."

She was about to explain the CWP to George when there was a knock at the door. "Come in!" George said.

Will poked his head through the door. "Is everyone decent? Oh, hi, Nancy! How's it going?" He walked over and kissed George's cheek.

"Okay, thanks," Nancy said, happy to see that the disturbing note hadn't changed anything between Will and George. They really belonged together.

"I came by hoping I could drag George out of her room to the Cave for a while," Will said. "You're welcome to come along, too." He smiled at Nancy.

"Thanks. That sounds like fun," Nancy said wistfully. Just watching George and Will together made her think of Jake. She had an overwhelming urge to cancel all her plans—for that night, for the whole weekend—just so she could see him. "But I can't."

"Are you sure?" George asked, standing up and grabbing a jacket from her closet.

Nancy nodded. "Yes. But you guys have a great time, okay?"

"We will. Ready?" Will turned to George.

She took his hand. "You sure you want to go to the Cave? Why don't we go somewhere where we can get a real meal?"

"Like the Bumblebee?" Will asked. "Mashed potatoes, anyone?"

"Now you're talking." George smiled at Nancy. "I'll see you tomorrow, okay? Thanks for coming over!"

"Oh, of course," Nancy said. "Sorry it took me so long. Hey, is it okay if I hang out here for a second? I need to make a phone call."

"Sure, as long as it's not long distance," George teased.

"As if I would!" Nancy laughed.

George and Will left the room, and she grabbed the phone off George's dresser. It was stupid to spend her Friday night by herself working on her article when she could be with Jake!

Maybe it wasn't too late—they could still catch a quick dinner together. She dialed his apartment's phone number. After four rings, the answering machine picked up. "Hello, and thanks for calling," Jake's voice greeted her. "Jake, Nick, and Dennis aren't home right now. Okay, maybe we are. Anyway, just leave a message, and we'll get back to you as soon as we—"

Nancy hung up the phone, feeling dejected. Jake had apparently found another way to spend his Friday night. Now she had to go through with her original plan—without him.

She couldn't imagine a worse way to spend her night than sitting around, missing Jake. Knowing it was all her fault didn't help.

"I can pick up my little brother, but that's about it," Eileen told Bess. "And he's only four."

Bess shrugged. "It would probably take all the Kappas to lift Holly's car, and we can't all fit on the porch at the same time."

It was Friday night, and Casey, Eileen, Bess, and Holly were hanging out at the Kappa house after dinner. As fun as the evening was, Casey hadn't been able to relax and enjoy herself. She had only one thing on her mind: Charley's proposal. She wanted to call him. She missed talking with him, but he didn't want her to call until she had an answer, and she didn't have one for him.

"Then what are we going to do? I have to drive my car sometime this weekend," Holly said. "And I thought you said you were going to find ten guys to help us."

Bess looked sheepish. "I've been trying, but no luck."

"I know what we should do," Eileen said. "Go over to the weight room at the gym. That's where to find the strongest guys on campus."

"And you think we can just ask some strong guys to help, and they will?" Holly asked. "Why would they want to?"

"Because someone who's extremely charming and likable is going to ask them, that's why," Eileen said confidently. She turned to Bess, who was stretched out on the couch.

"Why are you looking at me?" Bess asked. "No—oh, no." She sat up straight.

"But, Bess, you're perfect for the job," Holly said enthusiastically. "Don't you think so, Casey?"

Casey nodded.

"Casey, you're so quiet. Is everything okay?" Eileen asked.

"Sure," Casey said. She tried to smile. Keeping Charley's proposal from everyone was getting harder and harder. She could talk about it with Bess, but Bess was only one person. And Bess thought Charley was the greatest guy in the universe.

She'd tried to bring it up with Stephanie, but

her roommate was too obsessed with talking about her stepmother's visit.

"Really? Well, what do you think of our plan, Casey? Bess saunters into the weight room and says, 'So, how'd you like to pick me—I mean, my friend's car—up?' " Eileen joked.

Holly laughed. "That I want to see. Can someone follow her with a camera? What do you say, Casey?"

"I'm sorry, Holly. I didn't hear you," Casey confessed.

"You've seemed really down all night," Eileen commented. "What's going on?"

"Is it Charley?" Holly asked. "Since he just left, you probably miss him a lot, huh?"

"I do," Casey said. "We had a great time." Casey paused and then went on. "So great that he actually asked me to marry him before I took him to the airport."

"What!" Eileen and Holly cried.

"How could you not tell us that until today?" Holly demanded.

"That's great!" Eileen exclaimed. "Isn't it?"

Casey nodded. "But there are a lot of things to discuss before I can decide. He wants us to live in Los Angeles, for one."

"No!" Bess declared. "You have to be here for the next four years. I can't imagine this place without you!"

"Neither can I," Holly said. "Couldn't he move here?"

Casey shrugged. "Not really. His acting career is in L.A."

"Wow. It's so complicated," Holly said. "So what did you tell him?"

"That's just it." Casey sighed loudly. "I haven't been able to tell him anything. And he's getting really angry. He wants an answer!"

"Pretty major decision." Holly tapped her shoe against the floor. "Can we help you in any way?"

"Well, I don't know," Casey said. "I think Charley and I need to work this through."

"And that must be hard to do over the phone," Bess said.

"Exactly," Casey replied.

"Then I think you should talk about this face-to-face," Holly said. "Could you fly out there?" she asked, turning to Casey.

"Oh, sure. Just blow off all my classes, hop on a plane . . ."

"Sounds good to me," Eileen commented, smiling.

"Well, if leaving here's not an option, there's only one thing to do." Bess picked up the phone and held it out to Casey.

"Discuss it on the phone? Again?" Casey groaned.

Bess shook her head. "No. Call Charley and make him come back here!"

* * *

"Whew!" Stephanie threw open the door of Suite 301 and walked in, tossing her purse onto a chair in the lounge. "This has to be the longest night in history!"

"I take it you were out with your dad and Kiki?" Kara asked, peering out from under her blue canvas baseball cap.

"*Out* being a relative term," Stephanie complained, sinking into one of the large, overstuffed chairs. "If you call eating a stuffed pepper at the Souvlaki House going out for dinner."

"You went to Souvlaki House?" Kara turned off the television. "Why? I thought your dad was into the finer things in life."

"He was. Until he met Kiki and decided that life was one big adventure," Stephanie said. "They actually canceled our trip to the Bahamas for the holidays so we can go backpacking out West. It's going to be such a great *adventure.* As if I want to spend vacation *camping!* With the two of them! I'd rather stay on campus, which is probably what I'll end up doing.

"And after dinner? Get this. She wanted a tour of the campus. A tour! What am I, a tour guide? Anyway, like she doesn't know what's on a college campus—she only graduated last year or something," Stephanie fumed.

"What? How old is she?" Kara asked. "Twenty-two?"

"Twenty-eight," Stephanie said. "Same difference. Way too young to be my so-called stepmother."

"You sound like Cinderella," Kara commented with a laugh.

"Cinderella? Cute. That's really cute." Stephanie shook a cigarette out of her pack and lit it, inhaling deeply.

"Think about it. You're the long-suffering daughter . . . Kiki's the Wicked Queen," Kara suggested mischievously.

Stephanie glared at her, one eyebrow raised. "That's Snow White."

"Oh. Okay . . . well, maybe this isn't the best time to ask you this. But then again, maybe it is," Kara said.

"What?" Stephanie asked.

"I need your help on something," Kara replied. "It's a project for my psych class that Tim and I are doing together."

"Couples therapy?" Stephanie laughed. She had to pat herself on the back for that one.

"No," Kara said slowly. "Actually, it's about you."

"Me?" What could Kara possibly have in mind? "Not that I'm not a worthwhile subject for any kind of study, but—psychology? Are you trying to tell me something?" Stephanie asked.

Kara shook her head, looking a little nervous. "Not at all," she said quickly. "It's just that our report's supposed to be on today's

American family. We've decided to focus on stepfamilies, which you now seem to be a part of. So I was wondering, could you fill out our survey? Answer some questions? Talk about what it's like?"

At first Stephanie was tempted to say something about how there wasn't enough paper in the world for her comments on having a new stepmother. She had a million things she'd like to say.

But then she remembered who was asking her—Kara. And there was no way Stephanie wanted Kara to see how she felt deep down. That she was hurt, lonely, and confused. She *hated* the fact that all of a sudden Kiki was pretending to replace her mother.

But nobody would find that out—especially not Kara. Stephanie would have to be careful about what she said.

"I'll think about it, okay?" she told Kara. "Now I'm bushed."

"Great, Steph. Remember, don't do it if you don't want to," Kara said.

"Why wouldn't I want to?" Stephanie bristled. "It's fine. Just not tonight, okay?" She whisked off down the hall into her room and closed the door behind her.

Then, when she was all alone, she slipped off her heels, sat down on her bed, and started to cry.

* * *

Bess peered through the glass windows into the weight room at the gym. Considering it was Friday night, the place was fairly packed. Bess knew she ought to consider herself lucky because there weren't any major parties on campus that night.

Okay, she told herself. This shouldn't be that hard. Just walk in and head for the biggest guy.

She stepped into the room, smiling at a girl who was curling some free weights. Just behind her, a skinny guy with pencil-thin arms was struggling to lift a set of tiny barbells off the floor.

Sorry, Bess thought, walking past him. Maybe next time.

Then she saw them—a group of the biggest, strongest-looking hunks she had ever seen in her life, huddled together in a group, talking. They looked as if they'd just come from a calendar shoot. They could probably lift a bus, if they wanted to.

Here goes everything, she thought.

"Hi?" she said brightly, approaching them.

The tallest one turned around. He was wearing a blue sleeveless T-shirt with the words Wilder Weight-lifting Club printed on it. "Hi. Can we help you?"

Bess grinned. "Can you ever!"

CHAPTER 9

Reva had just gotten dressed Saturday morning when there was a knock at her door. She rushed to open it, expecting Andy. "What's the matter, did you miss me?" she joked, pulling the door open.

Darrell was standing there, carrying a canvas briefcase. He shrugged, his black leather jacket squeaking slightly. "Well, sure, but—"

"Oh, I'm sorry. Hi, Darrell! I thought you were someone else," Reva apologized.

"I'm the one who's sorry," Darrell said. "You called me three times yesterday, and I never called back. But the thing is, I've been completely swamped. I think I'm the only one on campus who doesn't have a broken computer."

"Well, come in," Reva offered, stepping

back. She felt a little flutter of nervousness on seeing Darrell. She still had to tell him that the bracelet he'd given her was too much, considering she only wanted to be friends. She went over to her CD player and turned down the music so they could talk.

"Thanks. I can't stay long," Darrell said. "But maybe I can take a look at your computer and give you a quick diagnosis. I probably won't be able to fix it until tomorrow, though."

"You're working the whole weekend?" Reva asked.

"I work whenever I can," Darrell said. "You saw my car—I need the money." He laughed, sitting down at Reva's desk and flicking on her computer.

"It starts to boot, but then it goes into this weird sequence," Reva explained, then told Darrell about the problems she was having with her computer.

"Okay, well—I wouldn't do any work on this if I were you," Darrell said, standing up. "I'd hate for you to lose something. I can come back tomorrow and run some tests, take it apart if I need to, but right now I have to take off. I have five other appointments this morning."

"Wow, you're booked solid," Reva commented. "Listen, Darrell. Before you go?

There's something I need to talk to you about."

Darrell looked concerned. "Is everything okay?"

Reva nodded. "Yes. It's just that—well, I opened the gift you gave me the other day." She took the small white box out of her top dresser drawer. "And it's a really beautiful piece of jewelry. It was sweet of you to give me something, to try to cheer me up. But the truth is—I just can't accept it."

"You can't?" Darrell asked, frowning.

Reva shook her head. "It's too extravagant a gift, considering that we're just friends. I mean, I'm seeing someone else—you know, Andy. And I don't think it's right to take this from you, because . . . well, it just isn't. I'm sorry. I really appreciate your thinking of me." She held the small box out to Darrell.

"And I can't try to talk you out of this?" he asked, taking the box from her and studying it briefly.

"No. I'm sorry," Reva said.

"Hey, it's cool. I only meant it as a friend, but I can see how it might cause problems," Darrell said. "I'll just have to find some other incredibly beautiful woman to give it to, I guess." He smiled faintly. "Not that I know any."

"You'll meet someone," Reva said encouragingly. "I mean, who knows? Maybe one of your appointments this morning will turn out to be with—"

"The woman of my dreams? No, I kind of doubt that," Darrell said, laughing. "Anyway, I'd better get going." He looked at the box once more, then shoved it into his pocket. "I'll come back tomorrow to see if I can fix your computer."

"Okay. Thanks a lot for coming by," Reva said.

"Yeah. Take care," Darrell said. He slipped out the door.

Watching him go, Reva couldn't help feeling a little sad for rejecting Darrell. He was a really nice guy; he deserved a girlfriend. If she wasn't already seeing Andy, she might consider dating him. But she was in love with Andy, and that was that. She wasn't looking for anyone else.

Darrell had taken the news pretty well; if he was hurt at all, he hadn't shown it. And now I have a clear conscience, Reva thought, picking up the phone to call Andy. He was supposed to pick her up to go to brunch a half hour ago.

Ginny Yuen knocked twice on the door to the garage that her boyfriend Ray's band, the Beat Poets, used for a rehearsal space. There was no answer.

"Ray?" she called, knocking again. She

thought he'd mentioned dropping by some time that morning for a practice session with Spider and the rest of the guys. But she didn't hear any music. Maybe they're just not here yet, she thought.

She pressed her ear against the door. To her surprise, it fell open.

"Ray?" she called again. She decided he was probably so wrapped up in working that he didn't hear her.

As Ginny walked into the garage, she noticed the lights weren't on so, Ray couldn't be inside. Then why was the door unlocked? Ginny wondered, flicking on the light switch.

"What!" she gasped as she took in the scene.

Spider's backup amplifier was lying on its side, dented and scraped. Ray's old guitar had been thrown on the ground. Somebody broke in here last night! Ginny realized with a shudder.

Well, at least all their important stuff was still locked in the van from their gig the night before at Anthony's, Ginny consoled herself. But it looked as though whoever had broken in wanted only to trash the place. Otherwise, they would have stolen the amplifier and guitar.

Ginny turned to go. She had to call Ray right away and tell him they needed a new lock on the garage.

That was when she saw it. "Stay Away from Chinks—or Else!" had been spray-painted on the left wall in huge blue letters.

" 'Stay away from Chinks,' " she whispered. Why would anyone write that?

"Oh, no. That's me!" she said out loud, a feeling of disgust surging through her as she made the connection. She was Chinese American. Whoever wrote the warning was talking about her!

Ginny glanced over her shoulder and looked around the garage, feeling very vulnerable and afraid all of a sudden.

Somebody had wanted to hurt Ray—all because he was dating her!

But who? It didn't make any sense! And if this was their first warning—what was the second going to look like?

She rushed out of the garage, her heart pounding. She wasn't sticking around to find out!

"So they agreed to do it—just like that? For free?" Holly asked, gazing at the six guys who were walking across the lawn toward the Kappa house on Saturday morning at around eleven.

"Well, not exactly," Bess replied, nervously chewing her thumbnail. She'd poured on all of her immense charm, naturally. But she'd had to throw something else into the bargain, too.

"What do we have to pay them?" Eileen asked.

"N-nothing," Bess stammered. Not in money, anyway, she thought. It'll depend on who ends up paying for the meal. Bess wondered how she'd tell her Kappa sisters about the bargain.

"Hey, Bess!" Greg, the president of the Wilder Weight-lifting Club called out in greeting. He was wearing a muscle T-shirt, shorts, and the same lifting sneakers he'd had on the night before.

"Good morning!" Bess called, waving to them. She looked at Holly out of the corner of her eye. How is she going to take the news? Bess wondered. Will I get kicked out of Kappa for this?

"So, this is the car?" Greg asked. "This little hatchback? Pretty light, it looks like."

"Hey, it gets me places," Holly protested, pretending to be angry.

"Chill! It's nice," one of the guys said, laughing. "But it doesn't do you much good up here, does it?"

Holly shook her head. "No, not unless I want to sit in it and listen to the radio."

"Can I join you?" he asked, smiling at her.

"Talk about parking," another guy added.

Greg laughed. "All right, men. Work first, fun second. We have our assignment. Everyone stretched and pumped?"

A chorus of voices answered, "Yes!" loudly. The six guys surrounded the car, evenly spaced around it.

They almost looked as if they'd done this before, Bess thought. Maybe Zeta had recruited them, too! Of course, great minds like hers and Paul's would think alike.

"On the count of three," Greg instructed. "One . . . two . . . THREE!"

Almost immediately, the car was lifted a foot into the air.

"Wow," Holly said. "Check out their muscles."

"I am, I am," Eileen said, gazing at Greg.

Bess smiled. Everything was going fine, so far. Of course, moving the car was the easy part. She glanced nervously at her friends as the guys carried Holly's car down the three steps to the sidewalk, then carefully set it down.

"One, two, three . . . everyone got their tire down? Release!" Greg grunted.

"All right!" Several of the guys gave each other high fives in congratulations.

"Excellent," Holly said, shaking her head in disbelief. "Now I can hit the mall, go grocery shopping—"

Greg sauntered over to her. "What are you planning to cook?"

"Oh, I don't know. I hadn't thought about it yet," Holly said.

"Well, don't spend too much time worrying about it. I'm pretty easy to please," Greg said.

"You are?" Holly asked.

Uh-oh, Bess thought. Here we go!

"Didn't Bess tell you? You and I have a date this week," Greg said.

"No." Holly turned toward Bess, her eyes flashing. "Go ahead, Bess. Tell me all about it."

"Well, um, see," Bess stammered. It had seemed like such a great plan at the time. "Since these guys were nice enough to agree to get your car off the porch, I kind of made some dates for them with the Kappa sisters— you know, it's only fair."

"It is?" Holly asked.

"Of course, we can always put your car back on the porch, if you'd rather have it that way," Greg offered kindly.

"No!" Holly cried. "I mean, I was just surprised, that's all. Of course I'd love to make dinner for you. How about tonight, Greg? Italian okay?"

"Which one do I get," Eileen whispered to Bess.

"Take your pick," Bess offered. "Anyone except him." She pointed to a tall, blond sophomore who'd already asked her out at the gym. She was wondering how to break the news to Paul. Well, it's all his fault we got in this situation in the first place, she reasoned. He'll have to understand!

"So, what time works for you?" Greg asked Holly.

"Oh, I don't know. Seven?" Holly said.

"I'll be here," Greg said.

Holly kept grinning at him, her jaw clenched. "I don't know how I'll get you for this, Bess, but I will," she muttered under her breath. "Can you imagine how much spaghetti this guy will eat?"

"Just use one of the industrial-size pots in the kitchen," Bess advised. "That's what I'm going to do when I have dinner with Tom over there."

"Oh, sure. Save the gorgeous one for yourself," Eileen muttered.

"Hey, I'm the one who went to the weights room all by myself," Bess said. "Don't I deserve anything?" She giggled. "But seriously, you guys, this is all in fun. They know some of us have boyfriends."

"Some of us do," Eileen said. "And some of us don't. Too bad the rest of the guys you stuck us with look like such Neanderthals. Well, here goes. Just remember, you're going to pay for this, Bess." Eileen nudged Bess in the ribs before calling out to a guy who was leaning against the trunk of Holly's car and staring at her. "What's your name?"

Bess gulped. Nothing like a well-executed plan to get the weekend off to a great start!

"So what's up, everyone?" Nancy asked, taking a seat on the end of the couch in the lounge.

"Absolutely nothing." Liz stretched her arms overhead. "I *love* Saturday afternoons."

"Me, too," Casey agreed. "In a couple of minutes I'm going to make the supreme effort of getting up."

"Why would you even consider it?" Stephanie asked, patting her mouth delicately as she yawned.

"I'm going to order a pizza," Casey said. "Anyone want in?"

"I'm going out to lunch in a bit, so no," Stephanie said. "But I admire your motivation."

"Nancy? You want some? I can get an extra large from the pizza place," Casey offered.

"No, thanks. I have to head out pretty soon, too," Nancy said. She was planning to go out in search of Jake. She hadn't spoken to him since Friday afternoon, and she was dying to see him.

The only problem was, she hadn't been able to find Jake. She'd called his apartment, the newspaper office . . . she was running out of ideas about where to look. They'd left messages for each other, but hearing Jake's voice on her answering machine wasn't exactly what Nancy had in mind.

She was prepared to blow off all her homework to spend the afternoon with him.

All of a sudden the door to the suite burst open, and Ginny rushed in. "You guys aren't going to believe this," she said, panting.

"What's wrong?" Liz asked, scooting over on the couch. "Sit down. You look really upset."

"I am upset. But I think I'm angry more than upset!" Ginny declared.

"What is it?' Nancy asked, looking at her suitemate with concern.

"It's—I don't know what it is or who it is," Ginny said. "But somebody broke into the Beat Poets' rehearsal space last night."

"You're kidding," Casey said. "Did they take the band's equipment?"

"No," Ginny said, shaking her head. "They didn't take anything, but they trashed the place and left a huge, racist message painted in bright blue on the wall. 'Stay Away from Chinks—or Else.' " Ginny looked down at the floor. "And we all know who the Chink is."

"What pigs!" Stephanie declared.

"That's awful," Casey said. "I'm sorry, Ginny."

"Thanks," Ginny said. "But I can't believe that someone's harassing Ray about *me*. Who would care that I'm Chinese, anyway?"

Nancy thought about the note George had gotten, warning her to stay away from Will because he was Native American.

She didn't know whether she should tell Ginny that she suspected Wayne French and the CWP group or not. Ginny was clearly frightened, and Nancy hated to add to that. She decided to wait until she had something to back up her suspicions, even though she was growing more and more convinced that Wayne was behind all the recent racist attacks on campus.

Maybe I'll pay him a visit this afternoon, she thought. If she could find Jake, they could go together. If she couldn't, she might just have to go by herself, as much as she dreaded interacting with someone like Wayne. Where had Jake said he worked?

"I know—maybe it was those skinheads who yelled at Pam and Jamal the other night," Reva suggested.

"Skinheads are totally horrible," Stephanie said. "They're all into white supremacy and—"

"No, they're not," Ginny interrupted her. "All skinheads aren't like that. Ray has this skinhead friend who's always going to peace rallies. For some people, it's just a look."

"Yeah, a lot of skinheads are nonviolent," Liz added. "I think there's even an organized group of them."

"Whatever. All I know is, if I'm out at night

in some alley, I don't want to run into one," Stephanie said.

"Since you've probably never even *seen* an alley, I wouldn't worry about it," Ginny quipped.

Nancy was glad to see that Ginny was trying not to let the threat get to her.

"True. Alleys are not my thing, fortunately." Stephanie flipped her long, dark brown hair over her shoulders. "I'd better get ready for my late lunch with Daddy. Maybe today we can go to a *real* restaurant. But with Kiki around, I wouldn't bet on it. We'll probably eat at the Bumblebee Diner." She stood up and disappeared down the hall into her bedroom.

"I'd better take off, too," Nancy said, sliding off the arm of the couch.

"Going to see Jake?" Casey asked.

Nancy nodded. "If I can find him." She wasn't going to tell everyone where she was really headed. She wasn't even sure yet if she had the nerve to go through with it. "Ginny, I'm really sorry about what happened. If you need to talk or if there's anything I can do, let me know, okay?"

Ginny nodded. "Thanks."

Nancy grabbed her car keys and purse. Paying Wayne French a visit wasn't how she'd planned on spending her Saturday afternoon. And she'd much rather go see him with Jake by her side. But she had to find out more about the creep who was attacking her friends, and she hadn't been able to find Jake all morning.

Besides, Wayne might be easier to approach one on one. How *will* I get him to talk to me? she wondered as she went downstairs. She hadn't given it much thought, since she'd assumed Jake would interview him instead.

There was probably only one way to get Wayne to open up, Nancy decided. And that was to pretend to think just as he did. As detestable as it sounded, Nancy was going to have to pretend to want to join his horrible group.

CHAPTER 10

"Table for three," R. J. Keats said.

Stephanie still wasn't used to the sound of that. For years it had been "table for two." Stephanie glanced at Kiki standing beside her in a tailored ivory wool suit. The woman could make even something as boring and conservative as an ivory pantsuit look good. Stephanie found herself almost envying her stepmother.

Almost. But not quite.

The host showed them to a table by the window at Les Peches. Stephanie had finally gotten her way, at least where the restaurant was concerned. It was a small victory, but she'd take what she could get.

And today she was getting shrimp cocktail.

"This is a lovely place," Kiki commented as

she snapped open her linen napkin. "Do you come here often?"

"As often as I can," Stephanie said. "But usually I wait until Daddy comes to town." She grinned at her father, who was sitting across the table from her.

"Aren't I lucky?" R. J. Keats replied with a laugh. "Come on, now—I'm sure some handsome frat boy has brought you here on a date."

"Well—more like I brought *him*," Stephanie joked. "Most of the guys at Wilder think that the Souvlaki House is haute cuisine." She glanced at Kiki out of the corner of her eye. "No, correct that—they think that ordering a burger with Swiss cheese instead of American is going out on a limb."

Not that Stephanie had been going out on any real dates—she just hadn't found anyone she was interested in yet.

Kiki looked up from the menu. "I can see why you wait for your father to bring you here. This is an expensive restaurant for a small town like Weston."

"It's not *that* expensive," Stephanie commented.

"Well, when you're in college, you have to watch your budget," Kiki said.

"Yes," Stephanie said. "Right." When your father made as much money as hers did, though, things like that were kind of irrelevant.

It wasn't as if she was in a work-study program or needed a part-time job, like some of her suitemates.

"Kiki worked her way through college, working full-time at an investment firm," R. J. announced. "It took her five years, but she paid her own way."

Well, whoopee for Kiki, Stephanie thought. "That's great," she said, forcing herself to smile at her stepmother.

"By the way," R. J. said, gazing at both of them appreciatively. "Have I mentioned yet how much I'm enjoying spending the weekend with both of you?"

"No," Stephanie said.

"Well, I am," R. J. said. "And here I am, having lunch with the two most beautiful women in the room. Stephanie, you look especially radiant today. I don't know how you do it, but you always find the most beautiful dresses."

"Good taste runs in the family, I guess," Stephanie said, smoothing her new black silk dress. At least, it used to, she thought, until Daddy got remarried.

"That must have cost a fortune," Kiki said. "Are you sure you can afford to buy designer clothes now that you're in college?"

"Why?" Stephanie asked. "What's changed?"

"Well, your tuition is very expensive," Kiki

said. "Your father's really stretching himself—"

"Darling, it's not—"

"No, R. J., she should know," Kiki
continued.

"Know what?" Stephanie asked. "Daddy,
you're not *broke,* are you?"

R. J. laughed. "Hardly!"

"But," Kiki continued, "he's spending a
great deal to pay for your education at Wilder.
And that means he doesn't have a lot of extra
money for things like new silk dresses."

Stephanie glared at her. "What are you trying to say, Kiki?"

"I just want you to be aware that running
up huge balances on your father's credit cards
isn't exactly helping him out," Kiki said. "It's
fine to use them, but just don't go wild." She
smiled sweetly at Stephanie, who felt like
punching her right in her perfectly white, probably capped teeth.

"Anyway, that's all that needs to be said on
that account," R. J. said with a laugh. "Sorry
for the bad pun. I do think that whatever you
spent on that dress, Stephanie, was well spent.
You look marvelous."

"Even if I went over budget?" Stephanie
snapped.

"I certainly didn't mean that you should stop
buying nice clothes. Sometimes you can find

great deals at discount department stores," Kiki recommended. "You'd be surprised."

Surprised? More like horrified! Stephanie didn't know where Kiki had bought her ivory suit, but it certainly wasn't at any discount store!

The waiter walked over to their table before Stephanie could even think of a way to reply. "And what will we be having today?" he asked Stephanie, smiling at her.

A horrible, mean-spirited stepmother, Stephanie thought. That's what we'll be having—for the rest of my life!

"I'd like the shrimp cocktail," Stephanie said boldly. "For an appetizer. And then the Maine lobster, please."

She handed the waiter her menu and gave Kiki a superior smile. She'd like to see Kiki try to change her order. Since when did anyone tell her what she could and couldn't buy for herself?

Nancy pulled over in front of French's Auto Body Repair Shop. She peered up at the garage, then got out of her car and surveyed the lot. Six or seven dented cars in need of repair were parked in front of the shop.

Here goes, she thought, taking a deep breath as she approached the small office. "Hello?" she called out, knocking on the door.

"In here!" a gruff voice replied from the garage bay.

Nancy turned away from the office and walked over to the garage. "Hello?" she said again. "Is Wayne here?"

The tall man she'd seen at the arts and crafts show appeared from behind a rusted-out car. Just seeing him again made Nancy's stomach turn over. She could still remember all the stupid, hateful things he'd said about African art. "I'm Wayne. Who are you?" he demanded.

"Hi. I'm Nancy," she said, trying not to appear rattled.

"Which car is yours?" he asked. "Wait—it's the blue VW, isn't it? It's not ready yet, but it should be on Monday or Tuesday."

Nancy shook her head. "I didn't come about a car."

"Then what? I'm pretty busy, you know," Wayne said, wiping sweat from his brow with the sleeve of his black T-shirt.

Nancy glanced around the garage. Cans of different-colored primer paint were stacked on the garage's shelves along with tools of all kinds. Anything was preferable to looking at Wayne. "Actually," Nancy began, "I came here because I wanted to meet you. See, I was at the arts and crafts exhibit over at Wilder the other day, and I saw what you and your friends did."

Wayne was staring at Nancy intensely, as if

he were trying to decide whether she was for or against him.

"And I have to say, I totally admire your dedication," Nancy went on in a hurry. "You really made a statement."

Wayne set down the hammer he was holding. "You think so?"

Nancy nodded eagerly. "Definitely. And I asked a couple of people about you. They told me your name and where to find you. So I just came to say, you know, if you ever need any help ... I'd like to be part of the group."

"Really?" Wayne looked suspicious. "What group is that?"

"CWP. You know, Citizens for White Purity. A friend of mine had one of your brochures," Nancy explained. "I was into that stuff back home. But since I came to Wilder, I haven't found anyone who really shares my beliefs," Nancy said.

"Yeah? Well, have you heard a lot about our group?" Wayne asked, leaning against the car.

"Not too much," Nancy said. "What do you guys do—besides break up stupid world art exhibits?"

"Well, right now we're basically trying to get the word out," Wayne said, sounding very proud of himself. "So we're going around looking for opportunities to let the people know who we are and that we're a force to be reckoned with, as they say." He chuckled. "And I think it's working."

"Like what?" Nancy asked.

"Let's just say . . . we had a very good week. Last Tuesday we harassed some people on campus—you know, one of *those* couples?"

Nancy nodded. Like Pam and Jamal? she thought. One of *those* couples?

"Now I've got the police on my back after the arts and crafts thing," Wayne continued. "They started asking me about these other attacks on campus—"

"Did you have anything to do with them?" Nancy asked.

"Why do you ask?" Wayne asked, giving Nancy a sly look.

"Well, to tell you the truth, one girl who's in my dorm was mugged," Nancy said. "And I was wondering if the CWP had anything to do with it because, basically, I can't stand this girl."

Wayne grinned. "Well, I wish I could say I did that. From what I've heard, whoever's responsible deserves a pat on the back. In fact, I've kind of been hoping whoever did that stuff shows up at our next meeting."

"So you don't know who did it?" Nancy asked.

Wayne shrugged. "I might, and I might not. I mean, I'm not into advocating real violence against other people . . . at least, not yet. We'll see what happens. But there are people in my group who might decide to express their feelings in a more powerful way ... if they decide to do that, it's not my fault."

"No, I guess not," Nancy said. But she was thinking, Yes, it is. You can't just incite people with angry and violent ideas and then say it's not your fault.

"So you'd like to join? Do you want to come to our next meeting?" Wayne asked.

Nancy was getting angrier by the second, but she managed not to show it. She didn't know how much longer she could put on the act, though. "Yes, definitely. But I'm late for something, so I'd better run. Thanks for talking to me."

"Want to leave your number so I can call you? You might want to join our next public demonstration. We have quite a few planned," Wayne said with a smile.

"I'll get in touch with you in a couple of days," Nancy promised. She hurried toward her car. Wayne French had to be the most repulsive person she'd ever had a conversation with. She couldn't wait to get away from him.

Maybe Wayne French hadn't personally been behind the attacks on Reva and George, but it sure sounded as if his CWP cohorts had carried them out.

The only problem was, Nancy didn't have any proof to tie Wayne or anyone else in the

CWP to the attacks. And until she did, her friends—and possibly some other students on campus—were still in danger.

"Tell me again. Why are we doing this?" Paul asked Bess early Saturday evening. They were standing in the parking lot at Anthony's, having just gotten out of Paul's car.

"Paul, relax! It's only a double date. It won't kill you," Bess said.

"It won't? Can I get that in writing?" Paul teased, pulling Bess toward him.

Bess's lips met Paul's in a passionate kiss. "Well, maybe," she said.

"Okay. You probably think that because I'm kissing you, I'm letting you off the hook for setting up this double date thing with Leslie and Nathan," Paul said, tracing Bess's chin with his finger.

"And you probably think that because I'm kissing you, I've forgiven you for putting Holly's car on the porch," Bess said.

"How did you guys get it off, anyway?" Paul asked.

"We have some very strong friends, and that's all you need to know," Bess replied with a grin. "Now, let's go inside—Nathan and Leslie are probably dying in there without us." She gestured to the front door of Anthony's.

"Great—dinner with two premeds," Paul said. "I hope the music's loud."

Bess hit his arm lightly. "Come on, it won't be that bad. Leslie's really loosened up lately."

"Yeah. Yesterday I think I saw one strand of hair slip out of her headband," Paul said. "I thought she was going to have a heart attack."

"So she's type A," Bess said, walking into Anthony's. "But she *is* loosening up. She can be fun. Anyway, you're spending the evening with me. Isn't that enough?"

"We'll see," Paul muttered, walking behind Bess toward the booth where Leslie and Nathan were already seated.

Bess smiled when she saw how pretty Leslie looked. She had actually worn her hair loose, and she was wearing a soft green angora sweater over a small white T-shirt and black jeans. "Hey, you guys—sorry we're late," Bess said.

"That's okay," Leslie said, sliding over in the booth so that someone could sit next to her. "Paul, you remember Nathan from the Black and White Nights party?"

"Sure. Hey, Nathan," Paul said politely, sitting down beside Leslie. "How's it going?"

"Fine, thanks. This place is great," Nathan said, looking around appreciatively at the small, funky café-style restaurant. "Especially when you consider that I've been holed up in the Rock all afternoon."

"You study on Saturday afternoons?" Bess asked. "Wow. That's dedication."

"No." Nathan shook his head. "When you're taking biochemistry, it's called a necessity. If I didn't, I'd probably end up last in the class."

Leslie shook her head. "You're too smart to end up last."

"Leslie." Nathan turned red.

Bess laughed. "It takes a brain to know one."

"Well, actually," Nathan said, "Leslie's the smartest person in the class, unless you count the professor."

"Please don't," Leslie said. "Any comparison between me and somebody over the age of forty is completely unfavorable. Anyway, what's new with you guys?"

"Not much," Paul said, "unless you consider our little war with the Kappas."

"Fraternity stuff?" Nathan asked.

Bess cringed. She was afraid Nathan was going to say something critical about the Greek system; he had a kind of disapproving tone in his voice.

"Yes. I'm in Zeta," Paul said.

"I really like your house," Nathan said. "You guys are doing a lot of stuff for charity these days."

"We're sort of trying to turn over a new leaf," Paul said. "Improve our image and all that."

Nathan nodded. "Yes, I always figured I'd

join a fraternity when I got here, but then I decided I didn't really have time. I kind of wish I had, though."

"Oh, I can see you now," Leslie teased him. "Hanging from the chandelier with one hand, and holding your biochem textbook in the other!"

Paul burst out laughing. When Bess caught his eye, he winked at her.

So there, Bess felt like saying. Leslie does know how to have fun after all!

Which was going to make being her roommate much easier. I wonder, Bess thought. If my social life rubs off on Leslie . . . will some of her superbrains rub off on me? It only made sense, didn't it?

CHAPTER 11

Where's the food?"

Jake pointed to a table in the corner, where chips, crackers, and hummus had been put out on paper plates.

"Thanks, man." The guy nodded at Jake and moved over to grab a handful of chips.

Jake leaned back against the wall. He didn't know why everyone kept assuming this was *his* party. He didn't even live at the off-campus house that Mike, his friend from the animal rescue group, and four other Wilder students shared.

Speaking of Mike . . . Jake looked around the crowded living room. He hadn't yet seen either his host or Chaz, who'd invited him.

He was starting to wonder why he'd even bothered to come to the party. But he knew why he'd said yes so quickly; he had wanted to get back at Nancy for blowing him off on a Saturday night. He was determined to have fun without her. After all, it was the only healthy thing to do when you were becoming a serious couple. You had to spend time apart, and Jake planned on having a great time flying solo.

Only his plan wasn't working very well. All he had done at the party so far was lean against the wall, sip flat seltzer water, and think about Nancy. And the six messages she'd left on his answering machine. Her reddish blond hair that he loved coaxing through his hand. Her blue eyes and the way they sparkled when she was looking up at him, about to kiss him. And her kiss . . .

Jake's daydream was interrupted as the front door banged open and Chaz, Mike, and Amy rushed in, laughing and out of breath. Behind them on leashes were two German shepherd dogs so thin their rib cages stood out prominently.

"We did it!" Mike shouted, raising his fist over his head.

Jake stared at one of the dogs as Amy reached out to pet him. The dog bared its teeth, growling at her.

"Careful!" Chaz warned.

"What did you do?" Jake asked. He thought the dogs looked a little too dangerous to be in the middle of a crowded party.

"These are the dogs we told you about the other day," Chaz said. "The ones at the used car lot."

"We did a rescue mission, basically," Amy said.

Mike opened the cabinet, took out two bowls, and got a bag of dry dog food from underneath the sink. "Okay, guys. Easy now." He filled the bowls and set them on the floor, still holding the dogs' leashes. "Man, they're so hungry they'd probably eat anything," he commented.

Jake watched them gobble the crunchy nuggets. He'd never seen dogs that were so skinny. "So you took them? Was the guy who owned the place around?" he asked Chaz.

Amy was busy getting water bowls for the dogs, and Mike was keeping close tabs on their movements.

"No. We waited for him to leave," Chaz announced as a crowd gathered in front of him. "He drove off, and we went in. We used bolt cutters to cut the chain lock on his gates. Mike managed to get control of the dogs, so Amy and I decided to let this guy know what a royal jerk he was," Chaz explained. He pulled a hammer out of the back pocket of his jeans. "Let's just say that he won't be getting *quite* as much for those cars as he wanted—not with all the broken windows."

Several people in the crowd laughed, but

Jake wasn't amused. Sure, the guy had abused his dogs—and he should be prosecuted for that—but did Chaz and Amy have the right to destroy his personal property?

"Oh, don't forget, everyone. Next week is the demonstration against the Wilder research lab," Amy announced. "You're all coming, aren't you?"

"Right on!" several people answered.

Jake had been planning all along to attend the protest demonstration against the lab, especially after seeing some photographs, supposedly taken at the lab, of the animals used in research projects there. But now that he knew what Chaz, Mike, and Amy had done to the used car lot owner's property, he wasn't so sure. Protests were one thing; wrecking property was another.

"You're still planning a peaceful protest, right?" Jake asked.

"Yeah, of course," Amy said.

"That's why we need all of you to be there," Mike announced. "Protests only work when there are hundreds of people helping you make your point."

"We're with you all the way, buddy," one student said.

All the way, Jake mused. Except for your extreme tactics. He'd still go to the protest, he decided. But if it was anything more than standing around, holding signs, and making speeches, he wouldn't take part.

"Do you want something to eat?" Nancy gestured to the glass display case and smiled at Anna.

"Well ... some popcorn would taste good," Anna suggested shyly. "A medium, please. No, make it a large." She took the container of popcorn from the clerk, and Nancy paid for her soda and the popcorn. "Where do you like to sit?" Anna asked as they walked into the theater.

Nancy stopped in the aisle, and they looked around at the crowd. "Looks like we'll have to sit up front there, by the aisle. Is that okay?"

Anna nodded. "Sure."

Nancy smiled. She couldn't believe how much Anna had loosened up since the first time she'd met her. Maybe because she'd lost her mother, she was very mature for her age. In any case, they managed to find a lot to laugh at together.

They took their seats and Anna held out the popcorn to Nancy. "Want some? I only have enough for the entire seventh grade here." She frowned at the full bucket.

"Sure. Thanks." Nancy took a napkin and a handful of popcorn. "So, how have things been since the other day? How's school?"

"Okay, I guess," Anna said. "How's school for you?"

Nancy shrugged. "Okay. I've been kind of preoccupied this week, so I'm afraid I haven't spent as much time on my classes as I should have."

"Preoccupied? Like with your boyfriend that you told me about when we were at the mall, you mean?" Anna asked.

Nancy shook her head, smiling. She only wished that were the case. "Not exactly. Just . . . some problems my friends are having."

"Did you work them out?" Anna asked, tossing a popcorn kernel into her mouth.

"Not yet, but we will," Nancy said. "Anyway, how's your dad?"

"It's the weekend, so he's happy," Anna said. "He usually goes out with his friends on Saturday night, so it's cool we had something to do together." She glanced around the crowded theater. There were still a few minutes left before the movie would start. "Oh, my gosh." She grabbed Nancy's sleeve. "There's Dean."

"Dean?" Nancy repeated.

"Right over there. Walking down the other aisle. Plaid shirt," Anna said. "He's in the eighth grade."

Nancy spotted a tall, good-looking boy sliding into a seat next to a row of other boys, who were laughing and shoving one another around. "Do you like him?" she asked Anna.

"No!" Anna said, her face bright pink. "It's just that—he's cute, that's all." She sighed.

"But you don't like him," Nancy teased.

"No," Anna insisted. "He's a jerk! I hate him."

"Uh-huh. Right," Nancy said.

Then she and Anna burst out laughing.

The movie started, and Nancy slid down in her seat to get more comfortable. Unfortunately, after the first five minutes, her mind started to wander.

Something had been bothering her ever since her visit with Wayne. Even if he and his group had been behind some of the racist acts on campus, did they really have time to commit all of them? The fact that Wayne didn't seem to know who'd perpetrated a few of the attacks worried Nancy. Or was Wayne just pretending to be in the dark because he didn't trust her?

Suddenly she remembered what she'd seen in his garage. All the cans of car primer spray paint on the shelves in several different colors. Of course!

Wayne could have sprayed Ray's garage space; Ginny had described a blue spray-painted message on the wall. And Dawn had told her that the Vietnamese student in Thayer had had his motorcycle spray-painted, too. If anyone had access to spray paint, and lots of it, that person was Wayne French.

Maybe her little visit to Wayne's garage was going to pay off after all. She'd have to run her idea by Jake later.

"Hey!" Kara called out when Stephanie walked into the suite Saturday night. "You survived another meal out with your father and stepmother."

"Barely," Stephanie complained. She slipped off her pumps and flopped into a chair. "If I had to listen to one more story about how wonderful Kiki was, I thought I was going to strangle my dad."

"Hold that thought, okay?" Kara rushed into her room and grabbed her psychology notebook off her desk. It sounded as if Stephanie was ready for her in-depth interview.

"Okay. So, you were saying?" Kara prompted, sitting on the couch. She glanced over at Stephanie, whose mood seemed to have worsened in the last minute.

She was frowning at her shoes. "And I suppose I don't need new shoes, either," she muttered. "And if I do, I can always get them at Discount Land."

"What are you talking about?" Kara asked, tucking her feet under a pillow.

"Kiki." Stephanie shook her head. "She's into things like saving money. As a hobby."

"Oh. Not exactly your style, huh?" Kara said.

"No. And not exactly my father's style, either," Stephanie complained. "I mean, she's having an incredibly bad effect on him."

"Things are changing between you and your dad?" Kara asked.

Stephanie nodded.

"Is it okay if I take some notes for my project?" Kara asked. "I promise I won't write about anything you don't want me to."

"Okay," Stephanie agreed. "As far as I'm concerned, you can write about it all. Maybe we can call it 'Stepmommy Dearest.'" Her mouth curled into a thin, tight smile.

"It can't be that bad," Kara said.

"It can. Trust me," Stephanie replied.

"Okay then. I wrote down some questions this afternoon that I want to ask you," Kara said.

"Shoot," Stephanie said, stretching her legs.

"First off, I was wondering whether you felt any sense of abandonment. Like, here goes your father marrying some other woman, and where are you?" Kara asked.

Stephanie didn't respond at first. Then she said, "My father hasn't abandoned me."

"No, I know that," Kara said. "But you could maybe still feel that way."

Stephanie only shrugged in reply.

Kara jotted down "no answer" beside her

question. "Next question. Okay, I'm para-phrasing here because I don't remember the exact quote. Freud said something like—all sons want to marry their mothers, and all daughters want to marry their fathers. What do you think about that?"

Stephanie stared at Kara. "I think it's really stupid."

"So that has no bearing on your feelings of jealousy, the idea that perhaps you're losing your father, that he's turning into someone else under the influence of your new step-mother—"

"You know, you're really insulting. Why don't you go offend some other poor student with a stepfamily?" Stephanie stood up, abruptly ending their interview.

"But—wait, Stephanie—I didn't mean anything." Kara fumbled for words. "I didn't mean to insult you! I just want to understand your feelings, so I can—"

"So you can write all about how lousy I feel and present it to your class next week?" Stephanie said angrily. "No way. Look, I don't know what you're learning in your psych class, but whatever you do, don't apply some half-baked theory you have to me!" She started heading for her room.

There goes my project! Kara thought, panicking. "Stephanie, please. You said you'd help me. And it's not just this project! I really want to know more about stepfamilies and how it feels and—"

"Then you'll have to find someone else," Stephanie declared. "It's a stupid topic, anyway!" She went into her bedroom and slammed the door.

Kara dropped her notebook and lay back on the couch, putting the pillow on top of her face. There goes my project—*our* project!

How am I going to explain blowing this to Tim?

CHAPTER 12

"How's it going?" Eileen asked Darrell Jones, who was sitting on the floor of her room, working on Reva's computer. He had taken the whole thing apart. "Any progress yet?"

"I think she needs a new circuit board, but I'm not positive yet," Darrell said. "Whatever it is, it doesn't look good."

There was a knock at the door. Eileen pushed back her desk chair and stood up. "It's Grand Central around here this morning. Isn't everyone supposed to sleep in on Sundays?"

Darrell laughed. "That's what I thought."

Eileen opened the door. Andy Rodriguez was standing in the hall. "Hey, Eileen," he said. "Reva around?"

"No, I'm sorry," Eileen said. "She went out with Nancy to pick up a newspaper."

"Already?" Andy asked. "How long ago?"

"Oh, about fifteen minutes." Eileen stepped back, and Andy walked into the room. "You know Darrell, right?"

"Sure. We met at Black and White Nights." Andy held out his hand, and Darrell looked up from his crouch on the floor and shook it quickly.

"How's it going?" he greeted Andy.

"Fine. What's the damage?" Andy pointed at the computer.

"I'm not sure yet, but probably kind of high," Darrell said. "Hey, I was wondering . . . I thought Reva mentioned something once about having her own computer business?"

"Yeah. We run it together, actually," Andy told him. "We have a service to help students with problems with software, the Internet, whatever."

"So you guys don't know how to fix systems," Darrell said. "Right?"

Andy nodded. "Not yet. We're learning and everything, but we don't do that kind of work."

"Uh-huh," Darrell said. Eileen noticed he was staring at the computer as he listened to Andy. He seemed to be thinking about something. "So do you guys have an office? Or do you work out of your rooms?"

"Actually, I have an apartment off-campus, and we run the business from there," Andy explained.

"It's the apartment with three phone lines. You can't miss it," Eileen commented.

"Yeah, three phone lines and lot of empty pizza boxes," Andy joked.

"I was just asking because I have some clients at Campus Computers that need help with the Internet. Maybe I could send some business your way," Darrell suggested.

"That would be great," Andy said. "Here—I'll give you our business address and phone number." He grabbed a Post-it note off Reva's desk and quickly scribbled the information.

"While I'm writing this, I'd better leave Reva a note. She's supposed to meet me for brunch in an hour. Remind her if you're still here when she gets back, okay?" he asked Eileen.

"Only if you bring me some home fries afterward," she replied.

"No way." Andy laughed. "Not that I wouldn't love to cater to your every whim, but we're going to the health food place. I could bring you some fried tofu?"

"No, thanks," Eileen said, making a face. "I'm a bacon and eggs person. I'll give her the note anyway, though."

"Cool. I'm going to shoot some hoops, so I'll catch you later," he told her. "Hey, good luck with the computer stuff," he said to Darrell. "Thanks for helping Reva."

"Sure. No problem." Darrell waved goodbye to him. A few minutes after Andy left, Darrell stood up. "I'll be back in a second. I need a tool that's in my car."

"I'll be here," Eileen replied, sitting down at her desk. She stared at the blank sheet of paper in front of her for a few minutes after Darrell left. Eileen had been trying to start a letter to her parents but couldn't quite get it going. She got up and paced around the room, thinking about her letter.

She was passing Reva's desk when she saw Darrell's tool kit sitting on top of it. She noticed the glint of something gold inside the tool kit. It was the bracelet, she realized.

Reva had told her about Darrell giving her a gold bracelet to make up for the one that had been stolen from her. She'd given it back to him on Saturday, and now, Eileen saw, he was still carrying it around in his toolbox.

Too bad he was so hung up on her, Eileen thought, lifting the bracelet out of the tool kit. The gold heart charm with pearls on one side and a tiny *R* in the middle of the other glinted in the sunlight coming through the window. Darrell was so thoughtful, Eileen mused. He deserved to find someone he'd be happy with, someone who didn't already have a boyfriend, like Reva did.

She placed the bracelet back in the tool kit. Better luck next time, Darrell, she thought.

"I'm not sure I'll ever forgive you for setting me up with that weight lifter dude." Holly frowned at Bess.

It was Sunday morning and Bess was having late-morning coffee and pastries with Holly at the Kappa house. Holly was sipping from a cup of coffee, looking half asleep in a pair of Wilder sweats and a Kappa sweatshirt.

"Wasn't Greg a nice guy?" Bess asked, brushing some powdered sugar from her lips. "You had fun, didn't you?"

"It was all right," Holly said with a shrug. "But I notice you didn't have *your* date yet. What did you do, set one up with everyone except yourself?"

"No. I told you, I have to go out with Tom. I just put it off a few days, that's all," Bess said. "I have to break the news to Paul first. He's not going to like it. Not that he could do anything about it, because Tom is, like, twice his size."

"Maybe he'll be as mad at you as I am," Soozie Beckerman complained, strolling into the kitchen. "Do you know what if feels like to have your whole Saturday night taken over?"

"I thought you wanted to go out with that guy," Bess said. She and Soozie had never been friends—in fact, Soozie had even tried keeping Bess out of Kappa. If her set-up date hadn't gone perfectly, Bess wasn't exactly sorry.

"I did! Only he didn't want to go out with *me*," Soozie said bitterly. "Can you imagine?"

Bess bit her tongue. Actually, yes, she wanted to say.

"He said, 'I'll call you sometime.' We all know what *that* means," Soozie complained. "That he'll never call me because he doesn't want to see me again."

"Oh. Sorry," Bess said, shrugging. "But you know, I'm not the one who got us into this by putting Holly's car on the porch. The Zeta guys are who you should really be angry with. Right?" she asked Holly.

"Well . . . maybe," Holly agreed.

"So what we should do, now that we've all had about eight cups of coffee, is think of things we can do to retaliate," Bess said.

"Bess is right. We have to get them back," Holly declared, sitting up straighter.

"You guys got us into this, and you guys get us out," Soozie declared, grabbing a doughnut off the table. Then she walked out of the kitchen.

"And that kind of wonderful volunteer attitude is what we all love about you," Bess muttered.

Holly swept her long blond hair over her

shoulder. "Forget her. I know what we can do! We'll have our weight-lifting pals put a truck on the Zetas' porch. Only this time, it'll be an eighteen-wheeler."

Bess giggled. "I don't think the porch would hold."

"What would get to them the most?" Holly mused. "How about an old-fashioned panty raid? Only it would have to be a boxer shorts raid!"

Bess groaned. "No way. Not interested."

"All right. I want this prank to go down in Kappa history," Holly added. "Or even better, Zeta history!"

The two of them stared at the table, concentrating. But Bess couldn't think of a thing. "I have an idea," she finally said.

"What?" Holly asked eagerly.

"I'm going over to Thayer to see if Eileen and Casey have any ideas," Bess said. "Want to get dressed and come with me?"

"Get dressed?" Holly moaned. "Walk all the way to Thayer?"

"Who says we have to walk? I mean, that is why we went on those dates, so you could use your car again," Bess said with a smile. "See? Maybe it was worth it after all."

Holly frowned at her. *"You* didn't have to cook three pounds of spaghetti last night."

* * *

"Oh—too bad. You just missed Darrell," Eileen said when Reva and Nancy came back to the room.

"Darrell?" Nancy said to Reva. "Uh-oh. Did your hard drive crash again?" She looked over at the disassembled computer Reva was inspecting.

"I don't know what it is, but my computer's definitely not working right," Reva explained. "Darrell came over to fix it yesterday, but he didn't have time, so he said he'd be back today."

"He's a really sweet guy," Eileen said, fiddling with a pen on her desk. "You know, I kind of feel sorry for him."

"Why?" Nancy asked, setting the two Sunday papers down on the desk.

"Because. He likes Reva so much," Eileen said, stretching her arms over her head and looking at Reva. "I mean, he's still carrying around the bracelet he gave you. I saw it in his tool kit. It's so pretty, with that little charm on it. He must have gone to a lot of trouble to buy something exactly like the one you had stolen."

"What do you mean 'little charm on it'?" Reva asked. "The bracelet Darrell gave me was plain gold."

"Yes, it didn't have a charm," Nancy said. She remembered picking up the bracelet and looking at it.

"Well, that's funny. I actually lifted the bracelet up and looked at it," Eileen told them. "So I know that the one I saw a couple of minutes ago had that little heart charm on it. And the heart even had the *R* engraved on it. Isn't that the bracelet you just gave back to him?"

Reva shook her head. "No. It sounds like the one Andy gave me. And I'm wondering how he'd have it. Isn't that odd?" She turned to Nancy.

Nancy nodded. "Definitely weird."

"Maybe he added a charm to it after you gave it back, hoping that you'd like the bracelet enough to accept it a second time if he offered," Eileen suggested.

Nancy shook her head. "No. Reva told him she's definitely not interested. If he does have the original bracelet, then where did he find it? And why wouldn't he give it back when he found out you'd been mugged?"

"He probably didn't find Reva's original bracelet until after he gave her the other one," Eileen suggested with a shrug. "And he wanted her to keep his instead of Andy's. Look, he's got a pretty massive crush on you. He might have decided to hide the original."

"Wait a minute," Reva said. "This doesn't make sense."

"You're telling me," Nancy said. She couldn't understand what Darrell had in mind, keeping Reva's bracelet from her. "Why does the guy have *two* bracelets for you when you won't even accept one?"

"No—I mean, it really doesn't make sense," Reva said. "Darrell has never even seen my bracelet from Andy, so if he did find it, he wouldn't recognize it as mine. And wouldn't it be broken, too?"

Nancy thought a moment. "Something's strange about all this."

"In what way?" Eileen wanted to know.

"Well, Reva was attacked on Tuesday night, but we didn't even find out about it until Wednesday morning," Nancy said. "And we all live in the same suite. How did Darrell manage to hear about it so fast?"

"Easy," Eileen said. "He dropped by to see Reva, and I told him. He seemed really upset about it, and that's when I knew how much he liked you."

"Did you tell him about Reva's bracelet being stolen?" Nancy asked.

Eileen shrugged. "I think so."

"I don't get what's going on with the bracelets," Nancy said. "But if Eileen saw one just like yours in Darrell's tool kit today, that means he must have found it somewhere. Which means ... I don't know. He *might* have more information about the mugging than we realized."

"How would finding my bracelet help?" Reva asked.

"It all depends on *where* he found it," Nancy told her. "There's an organization on campus that might be connected to your mugging. Darrell might have found your bracelet when he went to fix a computer for one of their members, I guess."

"What campus organization is into *mugging?*" Reva asked.

"The group is called Citizens for White Purity," Nancy explained. "They've been behind some incidents on campus, like the riot at the World Arts and Crafts Show when they trashed the African art and—"

"Those jerks? You think they attacked me, too?" Reva asked, looking furious.

Nancy nodded. "But I don't have any proof. Except—wait a minute!"

She didn't know why she hadn't thought of it earlier. "The guy who's the leader of the CWP has an auto body shop in town. I was there yesterday. Remember how bashed up Darrell's car is and how he wants to get it fixed at a repair shop? What if he's been working so many overtime hours so that he can afford to get it fixed at an auto body shop—and that's where he found your bracelet!"

"Okay, but then . . . if he did, why didn't

he give the bracelet back to Reva yesterday?"
Eileen asked.

"Andy was here," Reva said. "He probably
felt uncomfortable. Or else he felt embarrassed
because you were here."

"Well, why don't you ask him about it?"
Nancy said. "Can you call him later or something—suggest you two get together in private?
It can be at a public place, just make sure he
knows you won't be with Andy. Maybe then
he'll feel freer to talk."

"Okay, I'll call him. But right now I have to
meet Andy, George, and Will for brunch,"
Reva said. "Though I have no idea where ..."

"I hope your heart wasn't set on home
fries," Eileen said. "Andy left you a note to
meet him at the Copacetic Carrot."

"They have great egg-free omelettes,"
Nancy said.

"Want to come along?" Reva offered.

"I'd love to, but I'm going over to Jake's
to surprise him with a home-cooked brunch,"
Nancy said.

"I hope he likes toast," Eileen teased.

"Hey, I'm a great cook!" Nancy said, laughing. She grabbed the hefty Sunday newspaper
and headed for the door. "Reva, don't forget—
call Darrell later, okay? We need to figure out
this bracelet thing once and for all."

"I will," Reva promised. "Right after
brunch."

"Great. See you guys!" Nancy slipped out the door into the hallway.

Finding out about Reva's bracelet was important, and she wanted to know what Darrell would say. But seeing Jake was even more important. She couldn't wait another second to be in his arms.

CHAPTER 13

"What are you doing here?"

Before his sentence was half finished, Nancy kissed Jake on the mouth.

"Never mind," he said, pulling her into his arms for a close hug. "I don't care what the answer is after a kiss like that."

"Good." Nancy followed Jake into his apartment and tossed the Sunday paper onto the kitchen counter. "Because I've come to make you brunch. Where are Nick and Dennis?"

"They went out for pancakes. I was going to join them, but I just had this feeling . . . a beautiful woman bearing groceries was going to drop by my house and kiss me."

"Beautiful woman? Yes. Kisses? Yes. Groceries?" Nancy asked. "Do I have to do everything?" She walked over to the refrigerator

157

and opened the door. The fridge was completely empty except for a bottle of ketchup and a six-pack of soda. "You know, on second thought, maybe Nick and Dennis had the right idea. Should we go out for brunch?"

"How about if we hit the grocery store? That way we can spend some time together, and when we get back, I'll help cook. Deal?" Jake asked, taking Nancy's hand. "You know, I love that you just showed up on my doorstep."

Nancy looked up at him, smiling. "And I love that you were here. Have you been hibernating all weekend, just listening to me call your answering machine?"

"That's it." Jake nodded. "I was lying on the couch the whole time, just making you squirm."

"You weren't." Nancy frowned.

"No, of course not! It was just that every time I called you, you were out—"

"Likewise," Nancy said. "When I got home from Anna's last night, it was later than I thought. Then I called—and you weren't even here!" She hit Jake playfully on the arm.

"Hey, easy." Jake grabbed her hand and brought it to his lips. "I got home from Mike's party right after you called. But it was so late, I figured . . . what was the point."

"The point was . . . *this.*" Nancy put her arms around Jake's waist. Then she stood on tiptoe and kissed his neck, his chin, and his cheek.

He tipped her chin and kissed her passionately. Then he stepped back, brushing her lip with his thumb. "Excellent point, Drew."

"Thanks. Now, I guess we should get going before we starve." Nancy said.

"Starving might be okay," Jake said, "if this is the alternative." He grinned.

Nancy and Jake went outside and walked down the sidewalk to her car.

About ten minutes later, Nancy and Jake were strolling through the supermarket, randomly tossing items into a cart. "Do you like mushrooms?" Nancy asked as they stopped in front of the produce section.

"I don't like any food where half the species is poisonous," Jake said, making a face.

"I want to make some omelettes—what do you like in yours?" Nancy asked, examining a few tomatoes.

"I don't know." Jake walked up behind Nancy, slipping his arms around her waist. "What do you like?"

"Cheese, tomatoes . . ." Nancy replied as Jake kissed the back of her neck. "Whatever."

Jake laughed. "Doesn't seem so important now, does it?"

"No. In fact, forget brunch," she said, turning around to face Jake. He tipped her chin, and their lips met again.

Nancy stepped back from Jake and smiled.

"So back to the omelettes," Jake said teasingly, holding Nancy's hand as they surveyed the rest of the vegetables. "Where to?"

"I think it's time to hit the dairy section for some eggs, then we're outta here," Nancy said.

"Cholesterol, here we come!" Jake cried, pushing the cart with renewed energy.

Nancy laughed, hurrying to follow him through the supermarket as he wildly dodged other carts.

"So guess what I did yesterday?" Nancy asked as they loaded the bags of groceries onto the backseat of her car about fifteen minutes later. "I went to visit our pal Wayne French."

"You're kidding! You went without me?" Jake slid into the front seat and closed the door. "How was it?"

Nancy turned the key in the ignition. "Not the best way to spend a Saturday afternoon. And I would have gone with you if I could have found you. But maybe going by myself was good, because I kind of got him to open up. I really think he's behind everything on campus. Did I tell you that somebody left Ginny an offensive message about being Chinese?"

"No. Hold on a second. Don't go anywhere yet," Jake said. "Tell me."

"That's really all I know," Nancy said with

a shrug. "Someone spray-painted it on the wall of the Beat Poets' rehearsal space."

Jake frowned. "Charming."

"That's not the only news I have, actually," Nancy told him. "You know that guy Darrell Jones? Who likes Reva? I told you about him, right?"

Jake nodded. "I think so. Wait, is that the same Darrell Jones who works for Campus Computers?"

"Right. Well, remember how Reva had her bracelet stolen during the mugging? And no one's seen it—except Eileen saw it this morning in Darrell's tool kit when he was fixing Reva's computer. So I'm thinking . . . how did it get there?" Nancy started driving.

"He must have found it on the ground or something," Jake suggested. "I mean, if he likes Reva, there's no reason he'd steal it from her."

Nancy pulled out of the parking lot. "Okay, but wouldn't he give it back to her if that were the case? Say he found it at Wayne French's auto body place—"

"Why would he be there?" Jake shook his head.

"Because he got into an accident recently, and his car's all dinged up," Nancy said. "Like that car—right there!" She pointed to a car across the intersection, which had about as many dents as Darrell's. Whoever owned it had tried to spruce it up by painting over rusted spots with paint that didn't quite match the car's original paint color.

Paint, Nancy thought. Like all the spray paint she had seen in Wayne's garage.

But she'd also seen paint somewhere else, she suddenly remembered. In the back of Darrell's car. Could *he* have left that threatening message for Ray and Ginny? But why would he? No, Wayne must have done it, Nancy told herself. But how could he be in so many places on campus? He couldn't!

Nancy suddenly pulled over to the curb and stopped.

"What are you doing?" Jake asked.

"Something doesn't add up," Nancy said, turning to him. "Wayne and his skinhead friends harassed Pam and Jamal at the Underground late Tuesday night. At about midnight Pam told George. But that's the same time that Reva was attacked. So unless someone else in the group did it, Citizens for White Purity couldn't have been behind Reva's attack. And Darrell has a bracelet that seems exactly like the one Andy gave Reva. So he has to have been the one!" She hit the steering wheel with her palm. "Can he be behind everything else, too? I can't believe it!"

"Neither can I," Jake said. "I'm serious. Why would Darrell attack Reva? He likes her, you said. Anyway, he's African American. So why would he go around campus instigating a bunch of racist attacks? No, it has to be Wayne French."

Nancy turned to Jake. "Maybe it's both."

He shrugged. "Possibly. How about if we talk about it while we eat?" His stomach growled.

Nancy looked lost in thought.

"After we eat, then we can go find Reva and talk about what we think," Jake proposed. "Okay?"

"Okay," Nancy agreed. "So, what exactly are *you* contributing to this brunch?"

"I'll talk while you cook," Jake offered.

"Excuse me, but I think you said that *you'd* cook," Nancy reminded him.

"I did? When was that?" Jake asked.

"About half an hour ago. But don't sweat it. I'm the one who came over to make brunch for you, anyway." Nancy smiled at Jake. It was great to be with him again. If only this business about Darrell and Wayne French weren't bothering her so much.

"We have to get the Zetas back, and we have to do it soon," Bess declared.

"You make it sound like war!" Eileen laughed.

"Well, it is war," Bess said. "When we have to go around campus, recruiting muscle—"

"And then dating muscle," Eileen commented.

Bess laughed. "Holly's a little mad at me because the guy she went out with dumped her already. I told her I only set up the dates. I don't guarantee results."

Casey smiled. She was glad that Bess had come over to their suite that morning—it was great to see her. But as far as coming up with revenge plans for the Zeta guys, Casey was too busy thinking about Charley to think about anything else.

"Okay. How about this, you guys. We sneak in and change the clocks in every single room," Eileen suggested. "So they all go to their classes two hours late—"

Bess laughed, and glanced at Casey. "What do you think, Casey? Any ideas?"

Casey sighed. "Not really."

"Uh-huh." Bess drummed her fingers on the back of the couch. "Casey, you don't have to pretend with us."

"Pretend?" Casey repeated.

"That you're actually sitting in the lounge with us, thinking about revenge on the Zetas," Bess went on. "When we both know you're a million—no, make that fifteen hundred—miles away. You're thinking about Charley."

Casey nodded slowly.

"You have to call him and get him to come here," Bess said. "It's on your mind so much, you probably won't get anything done until you settle this."

"And no *way* will your professors accept that as an excuse," Eileen commented. " 'Sorry I couldn't do my homework—I was thinking about my boyfriend!' "

Casey laughed. "You guys are right. I guess I'll call him." She went into her room and closed the door, leaning against it for a minute, collecting her thoughts. Bess was right. They couldn't make this decision in a couple of long-distance phone calls. It was too important.

She sat at her desk and punched in his number. "Hi, Charley!" she said excitedly when he answered the phone. "It's so good to hear your voice. I've really missed you."

"Hey," he said. "I've missed you, too."

"Charley, I want to talk everything over with you," Casey replied.

"So, talk," Charley prompted.

"I don't want to talk on the phone anymore," Casey said. "Getting married is a huge decision, and I just don't feel comfortable making that decision during a bunch of long-distance phone calls. I need to see you, face-to-face." She stopped talking and took a deep breath.

"You're right. I'll call the airline," Charley said. "Maybe I can get on a flight tonight."

Casey smiled. "Are you sure you can get away? You were just here a week ago."

"It's easier for me to take off than it is for you, with school and all. Besides, I think I'm racking up enough frequent flyer miles to earn a trip to Europe," he said with a nervous laugh.

"Okay then. Well, call me when you know what time you'll get in," Casey said, her stomach in a knot. Now that Charley was actually coming to visit, she had even less of a clue what she would say to him!

Nancy looked around the crowded table at the Copacetic Carrot. She and Jake had just explained to Reva, Andy, George, and Will that they thought Darrell might be behind some of the attacks on campus. Everyone was sitting in stunned silence, staring at one another.

"But that's impossible," Reva said, shaking her head. "There's no way Darrell would try to hurt me."

"Yes, he likes you too much," George agreed. "And why would he care about me and Will?

"Look, I don't know what else to say, and I'm not even sure I'm right," Nancy said. "All I know is, Eileen saw your bracelet in Darrell's tool kit. *We* saw the paint in his car's backseat. I don't know why else he'd have your bracelet, Reva. The more I thought about it, what are the odds that someone we know would find it?"

"Well, maybe he found it on the path where I was mugged," Reva said.

Nancy shrugged. She knew Reva was anxious to defend Darrell because she thought he was her friend.

"You know, I gave Darrell my address the other day. So if he's the one attacking people of color, then I could be next in line, since I'm Hispanic," Andy joked. "Come on—as if Darrell would do that! He's black, okay? You should look into that group you mentioned earlier—"

"Wait a second." Nancy put her hand over Jake's. "People of color. That's the connection."

"Well, sure—we knew that," Jake said, looking puzzled. "But—"

"It's not just people who aren't white," Nancy said.

"You're right!" Jake said, looking into her eyes. "It's people who are in mixed race couples."

"Like Will and George, Ginny and Ray . . . Reva and Andy," Nancy finished. "You know, your joke might not be that far from the truth, Andy. If Darrell's really against mixed race couples, he could be at your apartment right now."

"True," Andy said. "He knew we were all

going out to brunch here at noon—so if he wanted to . . ."

"Come on." Nancy jumped up from her chair. "We've got to find out, one way or the other."

"I hope he's not there," Reva said, hurrying out of the restaurant behind Nancy. "Darrell? Why would he do something like that?"

"I don't know," Nancy said, getting into her car. "I really don't understand."

When she pulled up in front of Will and Andy's apartment, Nancy spotted Darrell's car right away, parked across the street.

Her heart sank. She hadn't wanted to be right. For some reason it was easier to hate Wayne and his goons than it was to hate someone she knew, like Darrell. Or thought I knew, she reflected, turning off the engine.

"Let's go," Jake said, closing the car door quietly.

Nancy and Jake followed Will and Andy up to the apartment, with George and Reva close behind.

Will started to unlock the door but stopped and looked down. Nancy came closer and noticed that the lock had been jimmied. Will slowly pushed the door open.

Darrell was standing in the front hallway, a panicked expression on his face. He quickly tried to hide the can of spray paint behind his back, but Andy rushed forward, pulled it away from him, and shoved Darrell against the wall.

"What do you think you're doing in my house, you jerk," Andy demanded.

"Hey—easy," Darrell said, squirming under Andy's hand, which was pressing his chest.

"Easy? I should go easy? After you threw Reva on the ground? I don't think so," Andy said, getting right in Darrell's face.

"Come on, Andy—try to be cool," Will said, attempting to separate them.

Nancy walked into the living room, where Jake, George, and Reva were now staring at the wall over the couch. The paint wasn't even dry yet. "Go home, Spics and Indians!" was printed in blue paint.

"How disgusting," Nancy commented, frowning.

"I'm washing that off right now," Reva said, starting toward the kitchen.

"No, we'll need to show it to the police first," George said angrily.

Will and Andy led Darrell into the living room, one on each side of him. They sat down on the couch underneath the racist message. "You think that's funny or something?" Andy said, pointing at the hateful words. "You get your kicks out of harassing and scaring people?"

Darrell didn't say anything. Reva walked

over to the side of the couch and he glanced up at her.

"You should be ashamed," she told him. "Pretending to be my *friend?* Saying that you *cared* about me?"

"I did," Darrell said sullenly.

"You have a real special way of showing it," George commented.

"Why did you do it?" Jake asked. "And don't waste our time trying to tell us you didn't. We know you did."

Darrell's face clouded. He seemed to be thinking over his options for a minute. Then he finally said, "I couldn't believe you'd go out with someone . . . someone who wasn't like us."

"Like *us?*" Reva repeated. "What does that mean?"

"African American women should be dating their own kind. You know what I'm talking about, a *brothah.*" He looked meaningfully at Reva. "What's wrong, aren't black men good enough for you?" Darrell said angrily.

She folded her arms across her chest and just glared at him.

"I really liked you. When you wouldn't get involved with me, it made me angry that you weren't dating someone black. And then I read the newspaper article about Citizens for White Purity being on campus and encouraging attacks against anyone who wasn't white." Darrell frowned. "Even though I hated what they were saying, I thought I could use it to scare you into breaking up with Andy. I figured you'd get a chance to see what it could be like for you by dating him. There are lots of Wayne Frenches in the world."

Nancy looked over at Reva and saw that she was livid with rage. "That is the stupidest, most convoluted way of thinking I've ever heard."

Darrell got a defensive look on his face. "Well, I also knew everyone would think that group was behind all the attacks, and I thought maybe that would show people just how dangerous those people can be."

"You were hoping the CWP would be blamed?" Nancy asked.

Darrell nodded. "I thought I could lay it on them. All I wanted was for Reva to see that she should think about dating someone of her own color, like me, instead of someone like Andy. I didn't mean to hurt you, Reva."

"But that kind of thinking is just as racist as the CWP! And why would you keep attacking other people?" Will asked. "Innocent people like George? And Ginny?"

"Because I had to keep doing things to throw suspicion on that group so nobody would suspect me," Darrell explained.

"You are nuts, man," Andy said angrily. "You can't just attack people and get away with it. Especially my girlfriend."

"I can't believe you—attacking me just because of who I choose to date?" Reva asked.

"It's not right!" Darrell exclaimed. "You shouldn't date someone who isn't black. It's not fair to—"

"To whom?" Reva cried. "I have the right to date anyone I want to, whatever color he is!"

"You know, I hate to say this, Darrell, because Wayne French is an incredibly hateful, sick guy," Nancy said, "but Will's right. The way you're talking, you're just as bad as Wayne and the CWP."

"I'm calling the police," Jake said, picking up the phone from on top of the television.

"Darrell, I don't choose boyfriends or friends based on what they look like or what color skin they have," Reva declared. "I choose them because they're good, decent people I can trust and love. But you wouldn't know anything about that. Attacking someone to scare them away from a person they love—that's sick. And really sad, too."

Nancy stared at Reva, who was brushing an angry tear off her cheek. She couldn't agree more.

CHAPTER 14

Stephanie handed her father his leather briefcase. "So, Dad. I guess this is goodbye." It was Monday morning. She was standing outside the bed and breakfast where her father and Kiki had stayed. They'd just eaten a light breakfast, and Stephanie was helping her father pack the car while Kiki freshened up for the trip.

"It may be goodbye, but not for long," R. J. Keats replied. "We have our hiking trip coming up pretty soon."

"I don't know, Dad. Hiking, camping, eating nuts and berries . . . that's not exactly my idea of getting away from it all. And after exams I'm really going to *need* to get away from it all," Stephanie said with a loud sigh.

Not to mention get away from Kiki, she

added in her head. "Are you sure you need a double latte every morning, Stephanie?" she'd asked that morning at breakfast. "Wouldn't regular old coffee be fine?"

Stephanie prided herself on not liking regular old *anything*. Couldn't her stepmother tell that she was tampering with her identity?

"Well, we'll see. Once we send you some pictures and brochures, I bet you'll be raring to come along," R. J. said, putting his arm around Stephanie's shoulders.

"So the Bahamas is definitely out?" Stephanie asked, looking up at him. "Even if I already bought three new bathing suits?"

R. J. squeezed her shoulders. "Nice try, but yes, even if that."

For a second, Stephanie felt as if nothing had changed. She and her dad were joking around together, having a good time, just like they used to do, and—

"We'd better hurry if we want to make the flea market in Crandall," Kiki announced, flouncing down the front steps of the bed and breakfast inn.

"Flea market?" Stephanie was astonished. "Since when are you in the market for fleas, Daddy?"

"You wouldn't believe how many great antiques you can find there," Kiki went on, ignoring Stephanie's comments. "Really incredible steals. We can restore them ourselves, and you wouldn't believe how much money we save."

"Actually, I would," Stephanie said, nodding. After this weekend, she'd believe anything. Her father not only eating at dive restaurants like Souvlaki House, but rustic camping out West and now pawing through other people's used furniture?

Stephanie didn't care how frugal or nice Kiki was. If she kept coming between her and her father, Stephanie had no choice but to go into full-scale battle with Kiki for R. J.'s attention.

Maybe when she was around, Kiki could tell Stephanie what to wear, where to buy it, and how to pay for it. But she was leaving now. And as soon as their car was a speck on the horizon, Stephanie knew where she was going— straight to the mall!

"So Darrell attacked Reva and George and left that message for Ginny," Jake said. "And Wayne or someone in his group probably spray-painted Nguyen's motorcycle."

"Exactly," Nancy said. She and Jake were sitting in her room after morning classes. "Darrell's going to have to face charges for what he did. But the good news I got down at the police station early this morning is that Wayne's going to be arraigned on charges for what he did at the arts and crafts show. They're also investigating the other attacks and may be able to connect the CWP with those, too."

"Good. That'll put him out of commission for a while," Jake said, shaking his head as he smoothed Nancy's bedspread with his hand.

"Yes. The police told me jail time's a definite possibility, since he has a previous record," Nancy said. "Unfortunately, his group will still be around. I'm sure they're not going to go away anytime soon."

"We'll all just have to keep fighting their kind of sick prejudice. Maybe we can organize something to protest against their group," Jake suggested.

Nancy nodded. "Good idea."

"Speaking of protests, are you still planning to come to the demonstration against the Wilder Research Facility?" Jake asked.

"Sure," Nancy said. "Though what you told me about some of the animal rights people getting kind of radical . . . that worries me a little."

"Well, it worries me, too," Jake said. "But they really want this to be a large, peaceful protest so that lots of students on campus will get involved in the cause. I don't think they'll do anything to jeopardize that or turn people off."

"You know, it's going to be nice doing something together again," Nancy said, tapping Jake's cowboy boot with her shoe.

"Yeah. I kind of forgot what it felt like for a while this weekend," Jake teased.

"Well, maybe I can remind you," Nancy said, scooting closer to him on the bed so she was sitting right next to him.

"I don't know. It's a memory from way, way back," Jake said, running his hand along her cheek. "Did anyone ever tell you that skin's not allowed to be that soft?"

"No. Go ahead, though," Nancy said, smiling.

"Well. Maybe later. Right now I'd rather kiss you," Jake said. He leaned closer, and his lips almost touched hers. Then he stopped. "But before I do, promise me that next weekend you'll fit me into your schedule."

"It's a promise," Nancy said, leaning closer to him.

"No more phone messages left on my machine . . ." Jake ran his finger along Nancy's neck. "No more going to the movies without me . . ."

"Okay, okay! I said I promise." Nancy laughed. "Now kiss me already!"

"Come on, put it on," Reva urged. She was holding out her arm, waiting for Andy to put on her new bracelet. The police had seized the old one as evidence when they arrested Darrell—Reva had to identify it as hers.

As it turned out, Darrell had actually gotten

the bracelet repaired after stealing it. Why he had done that, though, Reva couldn't imagine. Then again, she didn't understand anything that Darrell had done.

"Here." Andy awkwardly fastened the clasp, then walked over to the window, staring out at campus.

"Wow. This one's even prettier," Reva said. "This is gorgeous, Andy. Thanks." She looked over at him. Something was bugging him, and he wasn't acting like himself. She joined him at the window. "What's wrong?"

Andy cleared his throat. "It's just . . . look. Maybe this isn't working out."

"What?" Reva asked. "What are you talking about?"

"You know. You've only been mugged and terrorized by some weird guy just for being involved with me," Andy said. "And maybe you want to get away from that kind of stuff because it could happen again. Maybe a relationship between us has too many risks. If you want to break up with me, it's okay. I'll understand."

"Good," Reva scoffed. "I'm glad you'd understand—because I sure wouldn't! Listen, Andy." She pulled him around to face her. "Darrell Jones didn't scare me away from seeing you. And nobody else is going to, either. I love you. I don't care what anyone else thinks or says about us or does to us. We know it's right. Don't we?"

Andy sighed, a look of relief on his face. "It's more than right." Then he put his arms around Reva and hugged her tightly. "And I'm never letting you go."

"You guys have to help me think of something," Bess pleaded. "Nobody at the Kappa house has come up with a good idea yet."

George took a bite of her hamburger. It was Monday night, and she, Nancy, and Bess were at the Cave for a quick bite to eat. "Maybe you could sign up the Zeta brothers for something, like . . . volunteering their services for some awful job—cleaning the sides of the highway," she suggested.

"They've probably already done that," Bess said. "They're into volunteering now."

"I don't know. All I can think of is a practical joke somebody pulled on my dad when he was in college," Nancy said. "It was his birthday, and the guys on his floor decided it would be funny to make it impossible for him to get out of his room by gluing his door shut. Which was really bad, considering it was finals week! He ended up climbing down the outside wall by tying a couple of bedsheets together!"

George laughed. "I can just see your dad doing that, too!"

Bess smiled. "You know, that might not be

a bad idea. Can you imagine doing that to a whole *house,* though?"

"I hope you have some spare time coming up," George joked.

"Actually, I don't," Bess said. "There's so much going on this week."

Nancy nodded. "I know. Are you guys going to the protest against the Wilder lab next Sunday?"

"I don't know if I can. I'll have to see how the studying goes. I've been using Sundays to put in time at the library." Bess sighed.

"Will and I are going," George said.

"Big surprise." Bess rolled her eyes.

"What?" George asked.

"You guys do everything together," Bess said.

"Is that a bad thing?" Nancy asked. "I feel like I never spend enough time with Jake."

"No—I mean, I'm actually envious," Bess said. "Because you and Will are so alike, and you share so many of the same interests, you can always do stuff together. That's really important in a relationship. You guys are one of the most perfectly matched couples I know." Bess grinned at her cousin.

"Yeah, I guess we are," George said with a shrug. Ever since the attacks against interracial couples, she had been thinking about her relationship with Will in a different way. She didn't love Will any less or care about his being Native American. She loved him deeply.

But she wondered if that kind of personal attack would ever happen again. Would it *keep* happening as long as they were involved?

"Hey—is this Girls' Night Out, or do you have room for another chair?"

George felt hands on her shoulders and looked up to see Will standing over her.

"Speak of the devil," Bess quipped to Nancy.

"He could probably *sense* that she was eating at the Cave," Nancy replied with a grin.

"Sure I could," Will said. He gave George a brief, tantalizing kiss, then sat down beside her. "Just as soon as I listened to the messages on my voice mail."

George laughed. Maybe things between her and Will would get rocky or complicated sometime in the future. But for right now, being with him was pure heaven.

NEXT IN NANCY DREW ON CAMPUS™:

Making choices. That's what college is all about. True or false? A, B, C, or none of the above. But sometimes you can't find the answer in a book. You have to search your heart. Charley Stern has popped the question, and now it's up to Casey to make her decision. The future is in her hands . . . but what does it hold?

Stephanie has her hands full, too, trying to get her father's attention. Money can't buy love, but who knows what a credit card can do? Nancy, meanwhile, has found a cause—animal rights—and a cause for concern. But the movement may be headed in the wrong direction, leading Nancy into a trap . . . in *Just the Two of Us,* Nancy Drew on Campus #12.

Christopher Pike presents....
a frighteningly fun new series for
your younger brothers and sisters!

The creepiest stories in town. . .

The Secret Path 53725-3/$3.50
The Howling Ghost 53726-1/$3.50
The Haunted Cave 53727-X/$3.50
Aliens in the Sky 53728-8/$3.99
The Cold People 55064-0/$3.99
The Witch's Revenge 55065-9/$3.99
The Dark Corner 55066-7/$3.99
The Little People 55067-5/$3.99
The Wishing Stone 55068-3/$3.99
The Wicked Cat 55069-1/$3.99

A MINSTREL BOOK
Published by Pocket Books

Simon & Schuster Mail Order
200 Old Tappan Rd., Old Tappan, N.J. 07675
Please send me the books I have checked above. I am enclosing $_____ (please add $0.75 to cover the postage
and handling for each order. Please add appropriate sales tax). Send check or money order–no cash or C.O.D.'s
please. Allow up to six weeks for delivery. For purchase over $10.00 you may use VISA: card number, expiration
date and customer signature must be included.
Name _____
Address _____
City _____ State/Zip _____
VISA Card # _____ Exp.Date _____
Signature _____ 1175-06

Now your younger brothers or sisters
can take a walk down Fear Street....

R.L.STINE'S

GHOSTS OF FEAR STREET ®

1 Hide and Shriek 52941-2/$3.99

2 Who's Been Sleeping in My Grave?
52942-0/$3.99

3 Attack of the Aqua Apes 52943-9/$3.99

4 Nightmare in 3-D 52944-7/$3.99

5 Stay Away From the Treehouse
52945-5/$3.99

6 Eye of the Fortuneteller 52946-3/$3.99

7 Fright Knight 52947-1/$3.99

8 The Ooze 52948-X/$3.99

9 Revenge of the Shadow People
52949-8/$3.99

10 The Bugman Lives
52950-1/$3.99

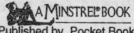 A MINSTREL® BOOK

Published by Pocket Books

Simon & Schuster Mail Order
200 Old Tappan Rd., Old Tappan, N.J. 07675
Please send me the books I have checked above. I am enclosing $_____ (please add $0.75 to cover the postage
and handling for each order. Please add appropriate sales tax). Send check or money order--no cash or C.O.D.'s
please. Allow up to six weeks for delivery. For purchase over $10.00 you may use VISA: card number, expiration
date and customer signature must be included.

Name _____

Address _____

City _____ State/Zip _____

VISA Card # _____ Exp.Date _____

Signature _____ 1180-06

Nancy Drew
on Campus™

By Carolyn Keene

Nancy Drew is going to college. It's a time of change....A change of address....A change of heart.

- ❏ 1 New Lives, New Loves......52737-1/$3.99
- ❏ 2 On Her Own.......................52741-X/$3.99
- ❏ 3 Don't Look Back...............52744-4/$3.99
- ❏ 4 Tell Me The Truth.............52745-2/$3.99
- ❏ 5 Secret Rules.....................52746-0/$3.99
- ❏ 6 It's Your Move.................52748-7/$3.99
- ❏ 7 False Friends....................52751-7/$3.99
- ❏ 8 Getting Closer.................52754-1/$3.99
- ❏ 9 Broken Promises.............52757-6/$3.99
- ❏ 10 Party Weekend..............52758-4/$3.99
- ❏ 11 In the Name of Love......52759-2/$3.99

 Available from Archway Paperbacks
Published by Pocket Books

- -

Simon & Schuster Mail Order
200 Old Tappan Rd., Old Tappan, N.J. 07675
Please send me the books I have checked above. I am enclosing $_____ (please add
$0.75 to cover the postage and handling for each order. Please add appropriate sales
tax). Send check or money order--no cash or C.O.D.'s please. Allow up to six weeks
for delivery. For purchase over $10.00 you may use VISA: card number, expiration
date and customer signature must be included.

POCKET BOOKS

Name _____

Address _____

City _____ State/Zip _____

VISA Card # _____ Exp.Date _____

Signature _____ 1127-09

Eau Claire District Library

NANCY DREW® AND THE HARDY BOYS®
TEAM UP FOR MORE MYSTERY AND MORE EXCITEMENT THAN EVER BEFORE!

A NANCY DREW AND HARDY BOYS SUPERMYSTERY™

- [ ] DOUBLE CROSSING — 74616-2/$3.99
- [ ] A CRIME FOR CHRISTMAS — 74617-0/$3.99
- [ ] SHOCK WAVES — 74393-7/$3.99
- [ ] DANGEROUS GAMES — 74108-X/$3.99
- [ ] THE LAST RESORT — 67461-7/$3.99
- [ ] THE PARIS CONNECTION — 74675-8/$3.99
- [ ] BURIED IN TIME — 67463-3/$3.99
- [ ] MYSTERY TRAIN — 67464-1/$3.99
- [ ] BEST OF ENEMIES — 67465-X/$3.99
- [ ] HIGH SURVIVAL — 67466-8/$3.99
- [ ] NEW YEAR'S EVIL — 67467-6/$3.99
- [ ] TOUR OF DANGER — 67468-4/$3.99
- [ ] SPIES AND LIES — 73125-4/$3.99
- [ ] TROPIC OF FEAR — 73126-2/$3.99
- [ ] COURTING DISASTER — 78168-5/$3.99
- [ ] HITS AND MISSES — 78169-3/$3.99
- [ ] EVIL IN AMSTERDAM — 78173-1/$3.99
- [ ] DESPERATE MEASURES — 78174-X/$3.99
- [ ] PASSPORT TO DANGER — 78177-4/$3.99
- [ ] HOLLYWOOD HORROR — 78181-2/$3.99
- [ ] COPPER CANYON CONSPIRACY — 88514-6/$3.99
- [ ] DANGER DOWN UNDER — 88460-3/$3.99
- [ ] DEAD ON ARRIVAL — 88461-1/$3.99
- [ ] TARGET FOR TERROR — 88462-X/$3.99
- [ ] SECRETS OF THE NILE — 50290-5/$3.99
- [ ] A QUESTION OF GUILT — 50293-x/$3.99
- [ ] ISLANDS OF INTRIGUE — 50294-8/$3.99
- [ ] MURDER ON THE FOURTH OF JULY — 50295-6/$3.99

Simon & Schuster Mail Order
200 Old Tappan Rd., Old Tappan, N.J. 07675

Please send me the books I have checked above. I am enclosing $_____ (please add $0.75 to cover the postage and handling for each order. Please add appropriate sales tax). Send check or money order--no cash or C.O.D.'s please. Allow up to six weeks for delivery. For purchase over $10.00 you may use VISA: card number, expiration date and customer signature must be included.

Name _____

Address _____

City _____ State/Zip _____

VISA Card # _____ Exp.Date _____

Signature _____ 664-16